Puffin Books

The kids from Koala Hills Primary School are growing up. Now they're in Grade Five, and this poses a whole new set of dilemmas:

- Who will have to kiss Kirsty in the school play?
- Is Peter really telling the truth about Disneyland?
- What happens when Mrs Smith gets hold of the Lovers' Club book?
- What happens to Mr Zeiner's beard at Carols by Candlelight?
- *What* is Factor X?

These intriguing questions – and more – are answered in this second very funny collection of stories about school life. Following the huge success of *I Hate Fridays*, here's another bunch of antics from Koala Hills Primary School.

Some praise for *I Hate Fridays*:
'*I Hate Fridays* is hilarious . . . You can laugh at yourself. And everyone else in the grade as well. It's top stuff.'

Paul Jennings

Also by Rachel Flynn
and Craig Smith

I Hate Fridays
I Can't Wait
Worried Sick

More stories from Koala Hills Primary School

Rachel Flynn

Illustrated by Craig Smith

Tania's copy, with all good wishes, Craig

Puffin Books

Puffin Books
Penguin Books Australia Ltd
487 Maroondah Highway, PO Box 257
Ringwood, Victoria 3134, Australia
Penguin Books Ltd
Harmondsworth, Middlesex, England
Viking Penguin, A Division of Penguin Books USA Inc.
375 Hudson Street, New York, New York 10014, USA
Penguin Books Canada Limited
10 Alcorn Avenue, Toronto, Ontario, Canada M4V 3B2
Penguin Books (N.Z.) Ltd
Cnr Rosedale and Airborne Roads, Albany, Auckland, New Zealand

First published by Penguin Books, 1992
10 9 8 7 6

Typeset in12½/16pt Cheltenham by Midland Typesetters, Maryborough, Victoria
Made and printed in Australia by Australian Print Group, Maryborough, Victoria

National Library of Australia
Cataloguing-in-Publication data:

Flynn, Rachel, 1953–
It's not fair, more stories from Koala Hills Primary School.

ISBN 0 14 034915 4.

1. Children's stories, Australian. I. Smith, Craig, 1955– II. Title.

A823.3

This book was written with the help of:

The grade-five and six students at Highvale Primary School, 1990, who told me a few things that they would not usually tell a teacher;

The staff at Highvale Primary School who told me some things that they wouldn't tell the parents;

Jean and her friends in grade five, who kept me informed about life at school;

Alastair, whose suggestions and comments are quite useful, and who designed the street-map at the front of this book.

From Rachel

For Henri and James

From Craig

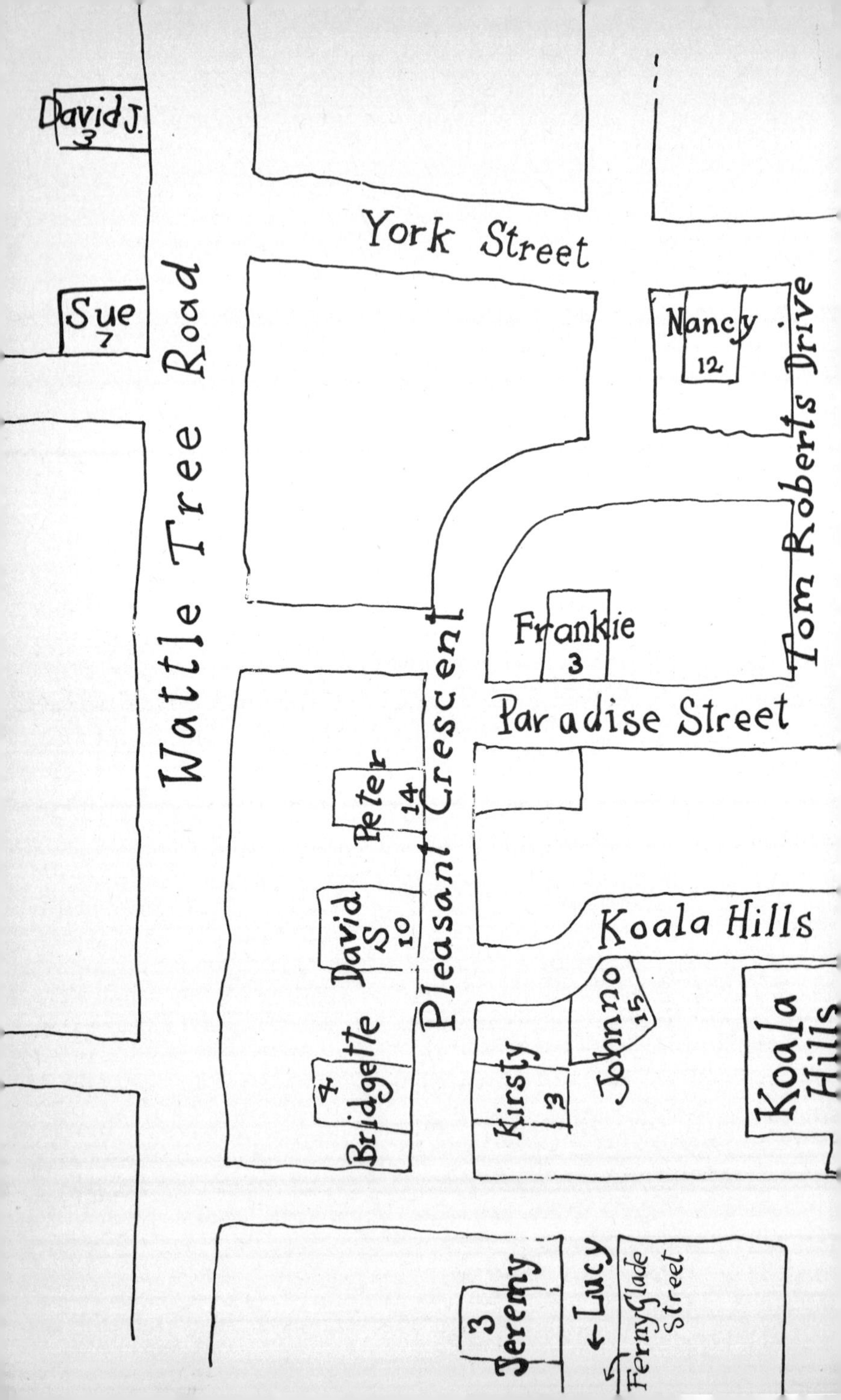

David J.
3

Sue
7

York Street

Wattle Tree Road

Nancy
12

Tom Roberts Drive

Frankie
3

Paradise Street

Pleasant Crescent

Peter
14

David S
10

Bridgette
4

Koala Hills

Johnno
15

Kirsty
3

Koala Hills

Jeremy
3

← Lucy

Ferny Glade Street

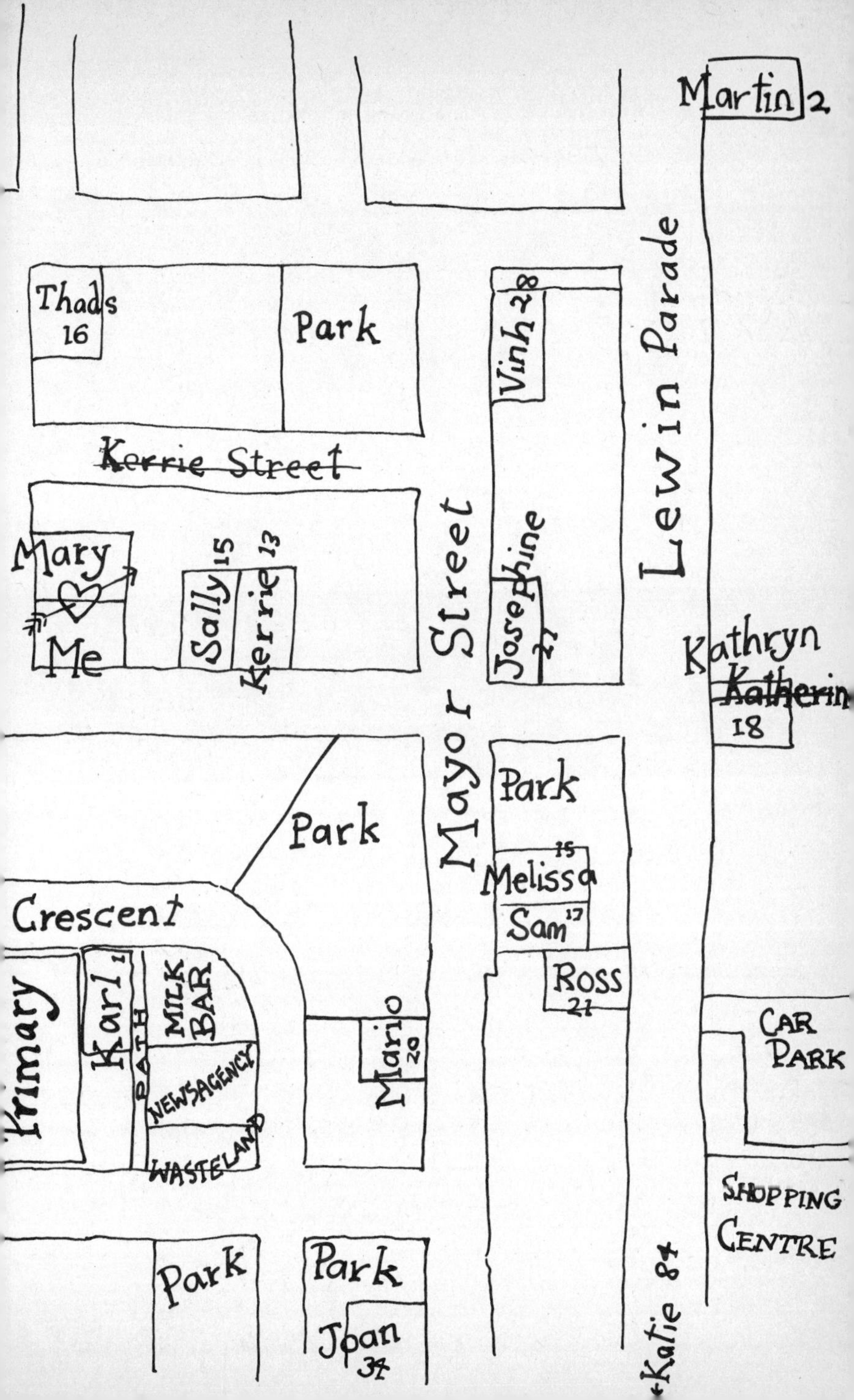

Martin 2

Thads 16

Park

Vinh 28

Lewin Parade

~~Kerrie~~ Street

Mary

Me

Sally 15

Kerrie 13

Mayor Street

Josephine 27

Kathryn

~~Katherin~~

18

Park

Park

Melissa 15

Sam 17

Ross 21

Crescent

Primary

Karl 1

PATH

MILK BAR

NEWSAGENCY

WASTELAND

Mario 20

CAR PARK

SHOPPING CENTRE

Park

Park

Joan 34

Katie 84

Martin Peters

TOP ROW Mario Marati, Johnno Jones, Josephine Wood, Jeremy Skinner, David Johnson, David Smith, Vinh Duong.

MIDDLE ROW Mrs Sheryl Smith, Ross Jenkins, Sam Lancer, Nancy Cleary, Peter Karlos, Karl Dreschler, David Pierce, Thadeus Antwerp, Frankie Morelli

BOTTOM ROW Melissa Dobell, Sally McKensie, Sue Lee, Joan Smith, Kathryn Chambers, Kirsty Dean, Katie Karachi, Kerrie Street, Lucy Williams
Bridgette O'Riley (absent)

Contents

It's Not Fair!

KOALA HILLS PRIMARY SCHOOL

Newsletter no. 1 3rd Feb.

From Mr Graves, Principal

I would like to extend a warm welcome to all the families in our school community, both old and new, and thank you to those generous and kind people who sent me charming cards and gifts as I lay in hospital over Christmas with two broken ribs and a perforated lung.

I was sorry to miss my usual camping trip to Rosebud, but made good use of my time planning a marvellous year's activities for the school.

Thank you also to those parents who watered the gardens and mowed the grass, although I was sorry to hear about Mr Antwerp coming face to fang with a tiger-snake.

I look forward to meeting you all at the BYO picnic on the school oval this Friday evening, when you will have the opportunity to meet your child's teacher.

Vice Principal and Prep
Mrs Marso
Grade 1
Ms Iris Waters
Grade 1/2
Miss Enza Karatsanis
Our old Grade 4 teacher.
Grade 2
Miss
Persephone Finly
Grade 3
Mr Warwick Woodroff
Grade 4
Mr Elvis Monroe
He listens to the races during class!
Grade 5
Mrs
Sheryl Smith
Grade 6
Mr Zachariah Zeiner
Library and
Integration
Mr Bob
Jergens
Phys. Ed.
Mr William Bollie
Art/Craft
Miss Melody Martiner
STAFF
Caretaker
Mr Heinz Dreschler
Secretary
Mrs Helen Lawson
Mum said that how come these two are at the bottom of the list when they really run the school.
Remember. School fees are due now

HELP NEEDED

We are seeking assistance from parents in producing our weekly newsletter. If you can type and use our office computer and are happy to spend Thursday morning duplicating, collating and distributing the newsletter, then please let Mrs Lawson know.

The canteen co-ordinator needs volunteers on Mondays, Wednesdays and Fridays. Note that the children of helpers are not entitled to free lollies.

Mr Jergens desperately needs assistance in the library with cataloguing, covering and shelving new books. The sooner this is done, the sooner your children may borrow them.

Dad said that if he looked like Mr Jergens then he'd be desperate too.

Working bees are held on the first Sunday of every month. We would like to take this opportunity to encourage all parents to come to at least two during the year. In exchange, you may have ten dollars of your child's school fees refunded.

Work which needs to be done includes: planting a cottage garden around the new art room (when it's finished), cleaning out drains and gutters, repairing the basketball backboards, relocating possums from possum-traps, re-surfacing the staff car-park and various other minor works. Workers will be provided with morning tea and a lovely BBQ lunch put on by the school council.

ADVERTISEMENTS

If you would like to advertise in this section, please send one dollar in an envelope with your child to Mrs Lawson.

Mr Tom Johnson, of Tojo's Autowrecks, can supply you with spare parts for your car: any make, any model, any time. Please phone for a confidential quote. 729 02145

These are all stolen!

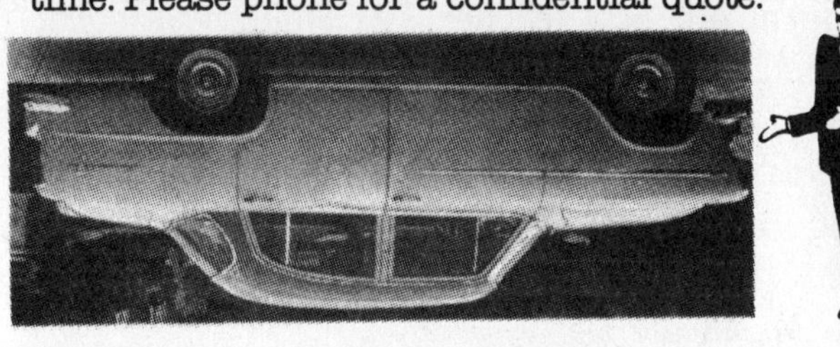

Mrs Dean, of 3 Pleasant Cres, will type your manuscript expertly and efficiently. Personal attention. 756 90324

Are you losing control of your money, your bankcard, your life? For financial advice ask the expert, Mr Percy Antwerp. Privacy guaranteed. 732 68127

Our ads bring results. This space could be yours. For information and advice, contact our advertising consultant, Mrs Lawson. Koala Hills P.S. 732 89105

Detention

by Kathryn Chambers

At first I thought our new teacher, Mrs Smith, was going to be really good.

When we got to school this morning, the first day of grade five, she made us all line up in silence. (Joan and I are good at that.) Then she let all the girls in and told us to choose a seat, in silence.

She kept the boys lined up and said that she'd had boys before and knew what they were like. What she actually said was that she'd 'ABSOLUTELY *HAD* BOYS' and already knew all the tricks they might get up to so they needn't bother thinking up any. She said this was the only warning they were going to get, and if any of them did anything she didn't like, then they knew what would happen.

It was then that somebody said, 'What?'

I think it was Thadeus. He believes that teachers are normal people and you can talk to them like you talk to your parents. Mrs Smith thought that he was being cheeky. She is new at our school and hadn't heard that Thadeus is good (for a boy).

She put him on detention straight away. 'This is what happens,' she said, 'and you can be an example to everyone.'

I smiled. It was only because I was so pleased to think that all the boys would be kept in order this year.

But Mrs Smith didn't know that I'm a good girl. 'So you think it's funny, do you?' she said. 'Then you can join him at detention.'

It was then that I decided she wasn't really a very good teacher.

Everybody was scared to even look at another person all day. We all worked in silence. Joan and I both had stomach-aches by lunchtime. I couldn't eat anything.

But do you know what happened? Just before hometime, Mrs Smith said that as Thadeus and I had done such excellent work all day, then she wouldn't make us do detention after all, and that tomorrow we would only have to work in silence for the morning.

If I were the teacher, I would let girls talk but not boys because they are too noisy.

'The Dictator'
Linocut by Thadeus Antwerp, 16 York St, Koala Hills (copies available 50c)

THE TEACHER'S SPEECHES

by Thadeus Antwerp

I had been looking forward to returning to school because Father had heard what a dynamic and inspiring teacher Mrs Smith is.

I had even brought Father's *Time Atlas of the World* (Comprehensive edition of 1968) for News. It weighs five kilograms.

However, my enthusiasm was truncated (cut short) when I was falsely accused of being cheeky, and sentenced to detention.

Mrs Smith began the day with a speech. This is how it went:

'Right, everyone listen to me. We're going to learn all about politics this year. We shall start with a DICTATORSHIP. I am going to be the DICTATOR. I have only one rule; that is, YOU DO WHAT I SAY. I've been teaching children like you for fifteen years, and I know what sort of tricks naughty little boys like to get up to.' (At this point she glared at all the boys with eyes like fibre optics.) 'Right, you've all been warned. That's the only warning you'll get, and if anyone does anything I don't like, they know what will happen . . .'

Someone said, 'What?' It wasn't me but Mrs Smith thought it was.

'Just what I was looking for,' she said. 'A nasty little boy of whom I can make an example. *You* will be in detention on Thursday until four o'clock.'

I was about to say that I didn't say anything, however all I managed was, 'But . . .'

'Don't "but" me,' said Mrs Smith. 'You will all work in absolute silence as from now.'

Kathryn Chambers turned around and smirked at me. Mrs Smith didn't like that either and put Kathryn on detention as well.

Everyone was too scared even to breathe. We did tests for writing, spelling, maths and reading. I got all my answers right and so did Kathryn. Mrs Smith announced that we would no longer have to go to detention as we had shown what excellent work we can do.

Then she let us all go home except for those people who had got most of their answers wrong. You know who I mean: Sam Lancer, Mario Marati, Johnno Jones, David Johnson and Nancy Cleary. They had to stay behind and listen to another speech, part of which I happened to hear as I was packing my bag in the corridor. It went like this:

'Right, everyone listen to me. I don't approve of children getting to grade five without being able to read or write properly. I can tell by your eyes that you are all perfectly intelligent so that means that you have not been paying attention for the last five years. LOOK AT ME WHEN I'M TALKING TO YOU' (probably to Mario). 'WHAT ARE YOU CRYING FOR?' (to Nancy). 'You will all have to do extra work at home till you come up to standard. Tonight you can write a list of all the people and animals who live at your place and what they eat for breakfast. DO YOU UNDERSTAND?'

They must have all nodded because she let them go. On his way out, Sam called Mrs Smith something, but I can't say what because I don't use bad language.

My list - I just did this one for practice — I love doing homework.

Mother:

Mother likes to begin the day with a cup of coffee while still in bed. Later she asks Father if she can have a spoonful of his muesli. He always says "Why dont you get your own bowl?" To which Mother always replies "Oh no I'm not hungry - I just want a little bit." Funnily enough this always makes Father irritable.

Father:

Father begins the day by making a cup of coffee for Mother. Then ... a bowl of muesli and likes to ... newspaper, when Mother ... him angry.

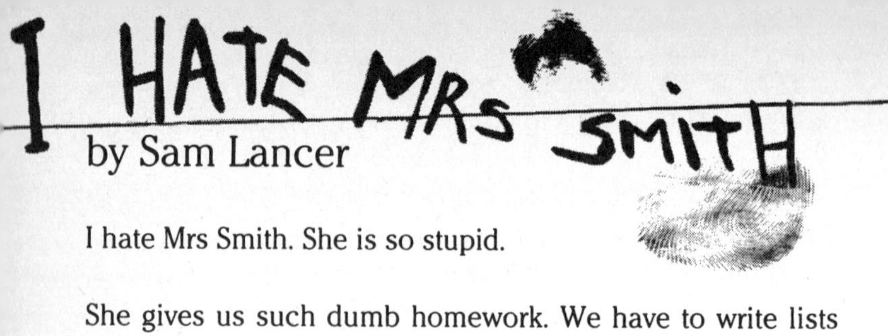

by Sam Lancer

I hate Mrs Smith. She is so stupid.

She gives us such dumb homework. We have to write lists of things every night like –

what you've eaten all day
what you watch on television
which things you have that run on electricity
food in the pantry that comes in glass

What's the point of writing lists?

I hate Mrs Smith. She makes us write a diary every morning. She says just to write anything we can think of. It's supposed to be about what we do at home.

It's none of her business. She just wants to find out stuff about us.

Mario wrote about his big brothers' gang doing graffiti and about finding a dead mouse in his dad's milk bar. It was in the freezer with the ice-creams.

I bet Mrs Smith tells all the other teachers about what we put in our diaries.

I just write about my dog Bruce. I wrote that he is a bull terrier and about the time he caught a burglar and bit his leg off. I wrote that he likes the taste of ladies better than men, especially if they have fat legs (like Mrs Smith).

I also wrote that my dad is a spy and has a special phone that only the Prime Minister can ring up on, and that he has to pretend to be a truck driver as a cover.

Mrs Smith believes everything we write. She is so stupid.

I haven't even got a dog.

'Getting Rid of Boys'   Drawing by Joan Smith. Year 5

Boys Are Despicable

by Joan Smith

The boys in our class haven't improved over the holidays. Some of them have even got worse.

Take Sam Lancer for instance. He used to be just awful, but now he is despicable. He makes rude signs at the teacher behind her back. He whispers awful things about her to his obnoxious friends, Mario and Johnno. He says terrible swear words. Sometimes I have to put my fingers in my ears so I can't hear them. He calls us girls 'morons' and stamps on our feet. I don't think we should have to put up with that, but I don't know what we can do about it.

The other boys aren't as bad as Sam, but that doesn't mean they're nice.

I was surprised to see Peter Karlos back at school this year. Everyone said he had died of embarrassment last December when his shorts came off at the school sports. But he isn't dead. He even looks more normal than he used to!

My best friend, Kathryn Chambers, said that boys have less brain cells than girls, and this is why they are remarkably stupid. She said that luckily there are some exceptions, but they're not in our class, or in our school, and possibly not even in Australia.

Kathryn said that if she ever bothers to look for a husband, she certainly won't be looking anywhere near Koala Hills. (That's here.)

Mrs Smith hates boys too, thank goodness.

A boy's brain – (shown actual size)

by Kerrie Street

Mrs Smith gave all of us a class list today. It has our phone numbers and addresses on it. She said it was so we could ring up and go and visit each other after school instead of talking in class.

I have put numbers next to all of my friends in order of which ones I like best. At the moment, Sally is my best best friend and Josephine is my worst best friend. It's hard to play all together because Kirsty and Josephine hate each other and fight all the time. The only thing they agree on is that they hate Peter Karlos, but Peter is all right really. Just because he tells lies and is awful doesn't mean we all have to hate him. My mum says that hate is a negative emotion that makes you feel sick.

Grade-five list Teacher – Mrs Sheryl Smith

Mark	Name	Address	Phone
☆	Antwerp, Thadeus	16 York St	73268127
6	~~Chambers, Kathryn~~	18 Lewin Pde	~~73281060~~
	Cleary, Nancy	12 York St	73682096
3	~~Dean, Kirsty~~	~~3 Pleasant Cres~~	~~75690324~~
	Dobell, Melissa	15 Mayor St	73248906
	~~Dreschler, Karl~~	~~1 Koala Hills Cres~~	~~73801618~~
☆	Duong, Vinh	28 York St	73684288
	~~Jenkins, Ross~~	~~21 Lewin Pde~~	~~73812336~~
yuk!	Johnson, David	3 Wattle Tree Rd	72902145
YUK	Jones, Johnno	15 Koala Hills Cres	73089447
	Karachi, Katie	84 Lewin Pde	73811780
★	Karlos, Peter	14 Pleasant Cres	73012547
YUK→	Lancer, Sam	17 Mayor St	72904667
5	Lee, Sue	7 Wattle Tree Rd	72931443
1	McKensie, Sally	15 Paradise St	73528910
YUK!	Marati, Mario	20 Mayor St	72068871
	Morelli, Frankie	3 Paradise St	73520900
4	O'Riley, Bridgette	4 Pleasant Cres	69336051
☆	~~Peters, Martin~~	2 Lewin Pde	~~72210078~~
☆	Pierce, David	1 Tom Roberts Dv	68354160
	~~Skinner, Jeremy~~	~~3 Ferny Glade St~~	~~67096657~~
☆	Smith, David	10 Pleasant Cres	73166702
2	~~Smith, Joan~~	~~34 Mayor St~~	~~72098811~~
	Street, Kerrie	13 Paradise St	69011336
	~~Williams, Lucy~~	~~28 Ferny Glade St~~	~~67302251~~
7→	Wood, Josephine	21 Paradise St	73527781

I have put a star next to all the boys I like. Thadeus is completely peculiar, but I like him anyway. He always has his pens lined up in order on his desk, and some people knock them off when they walk past, just to annoy him. He has his exercise books stacked in alphabetical order, and his coloured pencils numbered and labelled with his name and address. Kathryn says he has a compulsive personality disorder and will probably end up going mad.

Anyway, Kathryn keeps her socks up with elastic-bands. She says they have to be nine centimetres below her dress hem. She even has a line drawn on her leg so she can pull her socks up to the right place, which she does about a million times each day. Kathryn used to be my fourth-best friend but now she's my sixth-best friend. If she doesn't start being nicer soon then I'll put Josephine ahead of her, though Kirsty says we shouldn't even have Josephine in our group at all.

Sally has been my best best friend since we were babies and met each other at the health centre and I poked her in the eye. Kirsty is Bridgette's best friend, and Joan is Kathryn's, but we all play in a group, as well as with Sue Lee and Josephine, but they haven't got best friends.

Kathryn and Joan don't like boys, but I don't mind them because they're just people like us really, although most of them aren't very good at anything. My mum says boys improve as they get older. Joan says they only get worse. Kathryn says they've got brains like hot-water bottles and anything they may have learnt during the day leaks out through their ears at night.

by Peter Karlos

I've been thinking.

I wasn't a very nice person last year. I didn't really have any friends. I was awful.

I made some New Year's resolutions.

I've decided to be friendly. I've been practising at home. When I get up in the morning, I smile at Mum and Dad and even at my little sister, Sylvia. And do you know what? They smile back at me. (Not my sister though.)

I've decided to be nice to everyone, especially teachers. I like Mrs Smith. On the first day of school I gave her some flowers. I smiled at her and said how pleased I was to meet her. She smiled back and said 'Thank you'. My name was the second one that Mrs Smith learnt. The first was Thadeus but he was in trouble.

I said 'Good morning' to Joan Smith on the way to school today. She looked at me as if I wasn't there, but I'm going to say 'Good morning' to her again tomorrow.

I've decided not to say things about people, even if they are true, like:

Jeremy Skinner eats too much dinner.

Most girls are dumb but Nancy Cleary is dumber than most.

I've decided to make some friends. I think David Smith would be a good friend. He is really good at maths. I could help him at spelling and he could help me at maths, then we might be able to beat Thadeus and Kathryn in tests. David's got a swimming pool too and doesn't live far from me.

I'm really glad I've made these resolutions. I think I'll have a good time this year.

Telling Lies

by Kirsty Dean

Peter Karlos says that he went to Disneyland last school holidays, but nobody believes him because we know that he tells lies.

Peter says that he went in an aeroplane and stayed in a beautiful hotel. He probably only went to Queensland. And he says that he had rides on everything at Disneyland, but we don't believe him.

We know he tells lies because last year he said that he was changing schools, but he didn't. If he changed schools then he wouldn't be in our grade would he?

Last year, Peter said that his dad had a Mercedes, a Porsche, a Rolls Royce and a black belt in karate. But we know it wasn't true because we found out that his dad can't do karate.

So we know that Peter hasn't been to Disneyland. He tried to prove it by bringing some things he'd bought there, like a pack of cards and a T-shirt. But that's not proof. Someone could have given them to him, like his auntie.

Peter Karlos is pretending to be a nice boy this year. But he can't trick us. He tricked Mrs Smith, because she didn't know him last year, but we told her what he is really like. We told her what David Johnson is really like, too. He's also been pretending to be nice. She already knows what Sam, Mario and Johnno are really like. At least they don't pretend.

Peter said he could prove he went to Disneyland by getting us to ask his little sister, Sylvia. So we asked her and she said that she went to Disneyland as well. We don't believe her either. She probably only went to Luna Park.

We'll have to be very careful choosing boyfriends, because some of them might only be pretending to be nice like Peter does. I've decided to still have David Pierce for my best boyfriend and Martin Peters for my second-best one.

We're looking for one for Bridgette. I'm thinking of having David Smith for Bridgette's boyfriend. He'll be all right for her, but I wouldn't want him for myself.

Bridgette's not as pretty as me, but she nearly is. That doesn't matter though because David Smith isn't as good looking as David Pierce.

I told her that she wouldn't want Peter for a boyfriend because he tells lies, even though he is really rich.

Bridgette doesn't like boys who tell lies.

My NEW Girlfriend

by David Pierce

I have a new girlfriend. She doesn't come to our school. She goes to St Mary's. Her name is Mary as well.

She shifted into the house next door to our place at the end of the Christmas holidays. So did her mum and dad and three little sisters.

Mary has long hair which is usually tied up in things that hang down her back. She talks a lot. She first came into our place to ask when the garbage men came. She came in every day after that to ask more questions, and every day we played a bit.

On the first day we watched Dad making his sculpture. On the second day we played cricket with her three sisters and my one sister. On the third day I went with her whole family to the swimming pool. For the rest of the week we just hung around, and then school started.

Dad's Sculpture... He calls it 'Who Nose' .... I don't get it!

Mary gets home from school at about the same time as I do. She's pretty nice. She's also nice and pretty. It's good having kids next door. I like girls. You can talk to girls. I think I'll keep my old girlfriend as well, because I can see her at school and I can see Mary after school. It's all right to have two girlfriends if they don't know about each other, and especially if they don't even know about themselves.

I haven't told Mary that she's my girlfriend. I haven't told the other one either. But I've told Thads about both of them. He said he would be interested in meeting Mary's sisters. I said I would arrange it. So I did.

I arranged a cricket game for after school today. I started off bowling and Mary batted. She kept hitting the ball near Thads but he kept not seeing it. The first time, he was looking at Mary's little sister, Alice. The second time, he was looking at Mary's littler sister, Victoria, and the third time he was looking at Mary's littlest sister, Kathleen.

I couldn't get Mary out at all. None of the fielders were fielding. She retired at twenty runs. We swapped over and she bowled and I batted.

Victoria and Kathleen had stopped playing and gone inside, and Thads was explaining to Alice why the sky is blue.

Mary said that Thadeus is weird.

Seeing Miss Finly

by Joan Smith

I wish we still had Miss Finly for our teacher. She's the best teacher we've had. Mrs Smith is all right but she's not as nice as Miss Finly.

Mrs Smith makes us do too much work. She makes us be really quiet. She shouts at people just for putting their heads up (not me though).

She shouted at Kirsty one day just for talking during silent reading. All she did was tell David Johnson off for breathing on her. You should be allowed to stop people breathing on you. It's all right for Mrs Smith. She sits on her own, at a nice clean desk with flowers on it, directly underneath the ceiling fan. She doesn't have smelly boys sitting next to her.

I wish we still had Miss Finly. She only told people off for being really naughty. We saw her in the yard today. She was on duty. Kathryn and I, Sue Lee, Kirsty and Bridgette walked around with her.

Poor Miss Finly has Sam's little brother Lorrie in her grade. He is a total idiot. She also has Thadeus's little cousin Basil. He's like Thadeus only worse. He only eats white bread and butter for lunch. He's allergic to tap water so he brings his own bottle of distilled water. He is very thin.

This is what Miss Finly has to put up with in her grade. We think she ought to swap grades with Mrs Smith and have us again. She said she wasn't allowed to.

'YARD-DUTY' By JOAN SMITH Grade 5

We're going to walk around with Miss Finly every time she's on yard-duty. She'll like that.

by Kerrie Street

Four square is a good game because you can play it with three, four, five or six people.

That means Sally and I can play with Kirsty and Bridgette and Kathryn and Joan. Sometimes some of them don't want to play so we have Josephine Wood, but we'd rather not because no one can get her out. Also, if we have Kirsty and Josephine then it doesn't work because they don't like each other.

That's what happened today. We had five people and the person who is out stands out until another person goes out. Kirsty spent most of the time out, because every time she was in then Josephine got her out straight away.

Kirsty said that Josephine was picking on her.

Josephine said, 'So!'

Kirsty said, 'Come on,' to Bridgette and that she wanted to tell her something in private.

Josephine said it was very rude to tell secrets and she grabbed hold of Bridgette so she couldn't go.

Kirsty got up really close to Josephine and said, 'It's very rude to say "I hate your guts", so I won't say that, but I DETEST YOUR INTESTINES.'

Josephine told Bridgette to keep playing and Kirsty told Bridgette to come with her.

Then they both said, 'I hate you, I hate you, I hate you.' That's when the bell rang and we didn't get to finish our game.

Next play, Sally and I are going to play with Sue Lee and maybe even Nancy Cleary, but probably not.

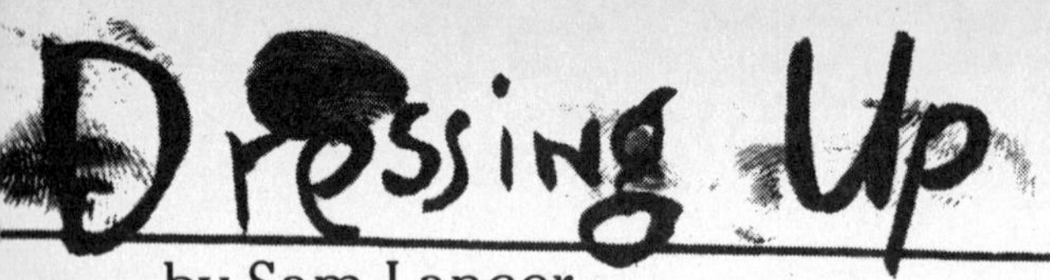

by Sam Lancer

This school is so dumb. We have an Easter-hat competition every year. We're supposed to make a hat and parade around in it like girls. Me and Mario and Johnno aren't that stupid. We decided to go on strike this year. We didn't even take the notices home. My mum never reads notices anyway.

The parade was really funny. The preps went first. Sylvia Karlos won because she is such a teacher's pet. Then came the grade-ones. Half of them were dressed as Ninja Turtles and weren't even wearing hats.

The grade-twos were next but my brother Lorrie didn't win because he didn't wear a hat because I told him not to. The grade-threes and fours were just so hopeless.

When it was our grade's turn, Johnno, Mario and me did silly walking and made all the kids laugh.

You should have seen Kirsty's hat. It took up enough space for four kids and had bits of stuff hanging off it down to the floor. I trod on some of it and nearly pulled her head off. She is such an idiot.

I don't know what happened after that because Mrs Smith went off her brain and sent me out. Who wants to see a stupid hat parade anyway?

~Me in our Garden~

by Kirsty Dean

I don't understand it. My Easter bonnet was the best, but Kathryn won the prize. Mine was much better than hers.

I started with Auntie Tizzie's wedding hat. It was already pretty, but I made it really beautiful by adding a pink fluffy bunny and lots of flowers made of crêpe paper. It still needed something, so I put on some curly streamers. It didn't look quite finished, so I tied on four large Easter eggs which hung down to my waist.

Each grade took it in turns to parade around the hall. Mr Zeiner, the grade-six teacher, played the piano. Mr Graves said things over the loudspeaker, Mr Monroe, the grade-four teacher, shouted at all the naughty kids, and Miss Martiner, our art teacher, chose the winners.

I don't know why she picked Kathryn because her hat wasn't as good as mine. Her hat didn't have enough things on it. It didn't even have any Easter eggs on it. It was even made from an old ice-cream container. Anyway, her mother made it.

The prize was awful. It was an old electric toothbrush left over from last year's school fete. Who'd want it? Not me!

Bridgette thought my hat was the best too. I gave her one of the eggs off it. I gave one to Joan too, and I gave Nancy Cleary one, but I didn't give Kathryn any.

Doing yard-duty

by Kathryn Chambers

Last Monday, Kirsty and Bridgette and Joan and I were helping Miss Finly do yard-duty. We usually walk ahead of her and find kids doing the wrong thing, then we tell her so she can shout at them. This saves her a lot of time looking for naughty kids herself. Besides, no one does anything naughty when they know a teacher is watching (except some boys).

We found all the grade-two boys writing their initials in the wet concrete that was going to be the floor of the new art room. We actually caught them doing it. We said, 'Caught you,' and grabbed two each by their collars.

But grade-two boys are pretty strong and they all escaped, all except Basil, but we hadn't caught him because he was just watching. Before running off, Lorrie Lancer pushed Basil backwards and he fell in the concrete right on top of all their initials. We were just helping him out when Miss Finly arrived.

'Well,' she said, 'what happened to you?'

'I fell over,' said Basil. 'The wind blew me.' He had wet concrete in his hair and all the way down his back. He had left a Basil-shaped hole in the concrete, and had blotted out all the writing.

'Well,' said Miss Finly, 'you'd better come with me.'

We told her what had really happened and offered to go and get Lorrie Lancer, but she just rolled her eyes around and said she didn't want to see him any earlier than she had to.

Poor Miss Finly has to have him in her grade every day.

Now Basil's got a rash because he's allergic to concrete.

KOALA HILLS PRIMARY SCHOOL

Newsletter no. 10 23rd March

From Mr Graves, Principal

What a marvellous term we have all had. The preps have settled in beautifully and it's nice to see the senior students setting such a good example for the littlies. Just last week I had the pleasure of seeing two of our most responsible students, Kathryn Chambers and Joan Smith of grade five, helping young Basil Antwerp of grade two, out of the newly laid concrete where he had been blown by a particularly strong gust of wind. At least the construction of our new art room is underway, even if that section of concrete will have to be redone.

He was pushed!

I was glad to see so many parents and toddlers attending our Easter-hat parade. I must apologise to Mrs Karlos about the breakage of her pearl necklace by one of Mrs Wood's babies. Apparently three of the beads which were swallowed have been retrieved and it is just a matter of days before the other two are expected.

Mum said that she had heard that the four people were Mr Graves and his wife and Mr Monroe and his dogs Rock and Roll.

Many thanks to the four people who attended the April working-bee. I hope to see a lot more of you at the next one which will be held on May 6th. Work to be undertaken includes weeding, pruning, spreading bark chips under the flying fox, cleaning graffiti from the office wall and making craft items for the fete to be held in November.

Dad said that if he had to work in a library then he'd be desperate too.

HELP NEEDED

Mr Jergens is desperately in need of assistance in the library with cataloguing, covering and shelving books that were purchased in February.

Prep teacher Mrs Marso would like to hear from parents willing to help with the language program (hearing preps read). Volunteers will receive a smile and tea and biscuits.

What sort of biscuits? Are they TimTams?

Mr Zeiner would like to know of any parents capable of helping with the production of the school play. He especially needs help with costumes, choreography, musical arrangements, training the singers and actors, and with organising auditions.

ADVERTISEMENTS

Mr Tom Johnson, of Tojo's Autos, can get you the very make and model of used car you want. 'I specialise in everything,' says Mr Johnson. These are all stolen. 729 02145

To Let: Beach house at Rosebud, close to amenities (shops and pub), $40 per night. Lovely views and sea air.
Contact Mr Tom Bodley (Snr). 733 13261

Mrs Dean, of 3 Pleasant Cres, will be available for seeing into the future and talking to the dead on Tuesdays and Thursdays from 10.00 till 3.00. Please phone for appointment. 756 90324

Mum said she is going to make an appointment and see if Mrs Dean can talk to our dead chook who died last year and was buried near the back fence.

Being Nice

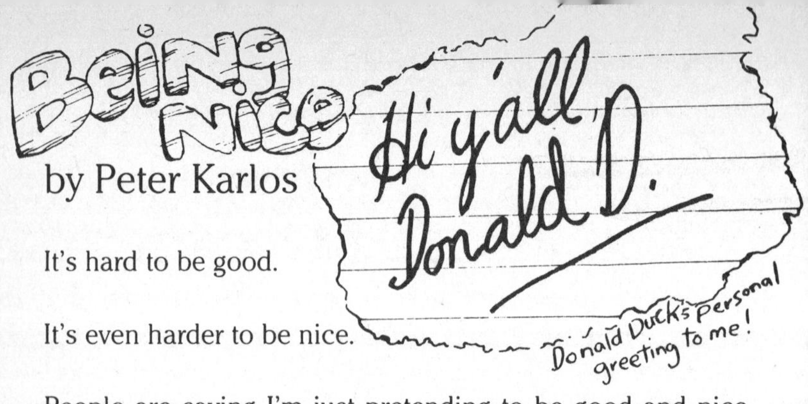

by Peter Karlos

It's hard to be good.

It's even harder to be nice.

People are saying I'm just pretending to be good and nice. They don't believe that I have made any resolutions. They don't even believe that I've been to Disneyland, even though I proved it.

I've been saying 'Good morning' to Joan Smith every day for weeks and she still hasn't answered me. All she has said is that she doesn't talk to boys.

I've been offering my playlunch to Jeremy Skinner even before he asks for it, but he never says 'Thank you'. All he has said is that I'd have to bring twice as much next week because he's a growing boy and can't be expected to survive on four chocolate biscuits till lunchtime. I didn't even tell him that all he is doing is growing fat.

I've been really helpful to Mrs Smith. I clean the blackboard, tidy up messes, hand out things and turn on the computer even before she asks. I check her work program and remind her about what we're doing next, but she doesn't seem pleased.

I was just marking the roll for her the other day because I'd noticed she'd forgotten, when she said, 'Thank you Peter, I'll do that.' She said it in one of those voices that doesn't mean 'thank you'. She made me sit down as if I was just like all the other kids.

Even though it's hard being nice, I'm going to keep trying. I haven't called any of the girls 'dumb' even though they are, and I haven't called Thadeus a twerp even though he is.

At least my friend David Smith likes me. When I asked if I could sit next to him he didn't say 'No'.

The Award

by Kirsty Dean

It's not fair. First I didn't win the prize for the best Easter bonnet, even though mine was the best, and now I haven't won the award for the most interesting and well-written true holiday story. Peter Karlos won it. Can you believe that? He wrote about going to Disneyland last January, and we don't even believe that he ever went.

Mrs Smith is going to give an award for the best true story after each term holiday. I bet I never win one. Bridgette doesn't think I will either.

At least my story was true. It started like this:

My Holidays by Kirsty Dean

Once upon a time there was a beautiful girl called Kirsty Imelda Dean. She had lovely golden curls and big green eyes which looked like pools of sea water against her soft creamy skin. She was a very sweet child and always kept her bedroom looking beautiful and tidy. Kirsty spent the holidays doing embroidery. She was very good at cross-stitch and had made a lovely embroidered mouse for her grand-mother's birthday.

It looked like this little cutey.

Mrs Smith said that I used 'beautiful' and 'lovely' too many times. If I was writing about her, I wouldn't need to use them at all. Then she said that she hoped I would do something more useful than embroidery during the next holidays.

I can't think of anything more useful. Neither can Bridgette. She wishes she was as good at it as I am. She spent the last holidays making little heart-shaped cushions with sequins sewn on them. All Sally did was collect Autumn leaves and flatten them in an encyclopaedia, and all Josephine did was go running around the streets. What could be more useless than that?

We had to read out our stories. It was very embarrassing for some people, like David Johnson, because some people can't write properly, and then they can't read it out properly either.

All David J wrote was, 'I didn't do nothing.' Mrs Smith said, 'That means that you *did* do something, David, so what was it?'

David said, 'Nothing.'

Kerrie spent the whole holidays drawing horses from different angles and colouring them in, and Martin Peters tried to train his pet lizards, Kylie and Jason, to go through a maze. What a waste of time.

Mrs Smith said that Peter showed a real talent for writing and she made us all clap. Nobody clapped very loudly, except Bridgette, who didn't realise what she was doing until I told her off.

We went to Disneyland during the last Christmas holidays. Some people don't believe it, but we did. My whole family went: Mum, Dad, me and my little sister Sylvia, aged four and three-quarters at the time.

My dad, who is a very important doctor, had to go to a conference about insanity in Los Angeles. He said we may as well all go and make a holiday of it. We left on January the 3rd. My Uncle Peter drove us to the airport and lots of relatives came to wave goodbye.

That's when the first bad thing happened. We tried to put our luggage in but our names weren't on the computer. First Mum and Dad had an argument with each other, then with someone behind the desk. All our relatives were sick of waving and smiling and had gone home.

Eventually we got on the plane and were on our way. Sylvia and I played Spot the Hijacker. She knelt up on her seat and looked over the back at all the people behind us. I was too polite to do that so I just carefully looked at people across the aisle without them noticing me.

Suddenly Sylvia yelled, 'There's one, he's a hijacker! He has black whiskers and glasses just like you said, Peter.' I tried to make her sit down but she started crying about the plane being blown up and all of us drowning in the cold, cold sea.

That's when the second bad thing happened. Mum blamed me for what Sylvia was doing and said that if I kept it up we wouldn't bother going to Disneyland at all. How could it have been my fault? I always get the blame for everything.

Pretty soon we arrived in Auckland and had to hang around in the transit-lounge before we took off again for Honolulu. We flew all night and slept nearly all the way. When we woke up we were given breakfast. Sylvia wouldn't eat anything so Mum made her drink some orange juice, seeing as we had paid for it.

That's when the third bad thing happened. Sylvia threw up. She threw up all over her clothes and her seat and her blanket and pillow and breakfast. I couldn't eat anything after that. Mum had to take Sylvia away and wash it off as best she could. She hadn't packed any spare clothes into our hand luggage. Dad told Mum she was stupid and Mum told Dad to shut up. The steward had to take Sylvia's whole seat away and bring her a clean one. She smelt terrible. I had to sit next to her.

We waited inside the airport for two hours at Honolulu, then got back on the plane to fly to Los Angeles. The stewardess asked us if we were going to Disneyland. Dad said, 'Maybe.' The stewardess said that if we were, then the best thing to do is to go at six o'clock in the evening and stay until midnight. She said that if we went in the morning then we would feel like going to sleep because it would be night time in Melbourne. She said that if we went in the evening then it would be less crowded, we wouldn't be tired and we would be able to see the fireworks.

When we got to Los Angeles Airport, we had to line up to go through Customs. The man asked us how much money we had and whether we had anything to declare. Mum declared that we had some Vegemite.

After we collected our luggage we went outside to catch a bus to our hotel. It wasn't like Melbourne at all. Lots of stretch limousines drove past, and buses came every two minutes. Each driver got out and told everyone where his bus was going and helped them with their bags. Sylvia was sick again, but only on the footpath. Nobody stood near us, not even Dad, because she still stank.

At last we got to our hotel and went to bed. The trouble was, we all woke up at midnight. Dad said it was because it was tea time in Melbourne. We eventually went back to sleep and this time we didn't wake up till two o'clock in the afternoon. Dad said it was because it was time to get up in Melbourne.

It was too expensive to eat in the hotel so we went across the road to a hamburger place for lunch, then we went to hire a car. At last we were ready to go to Disneyland.

It was quite a drive along lots of freeways. Even Dad was excited. Sylvia sang all the way. We got there at five-thirty. There was lots of space in the car-park. That's when the absolutely worst thing happened. We found out that Disneyland closes at six o'clock during January. The stupid stewardess was wrong. It was going to close in half an hour. Half an hour wasn't long enough to see Disneyland. Sylvia started to cry. Mum and Dad yelled at each other, and then they both shouted at us. What had we done?

We drove all the way back to the hotel. Mum and Dad didn't say anything. Sylvia cried all the way.

It was the most terrible day ever.

This story is completely true.

(We went back to Disneyland the next day at nine am.)

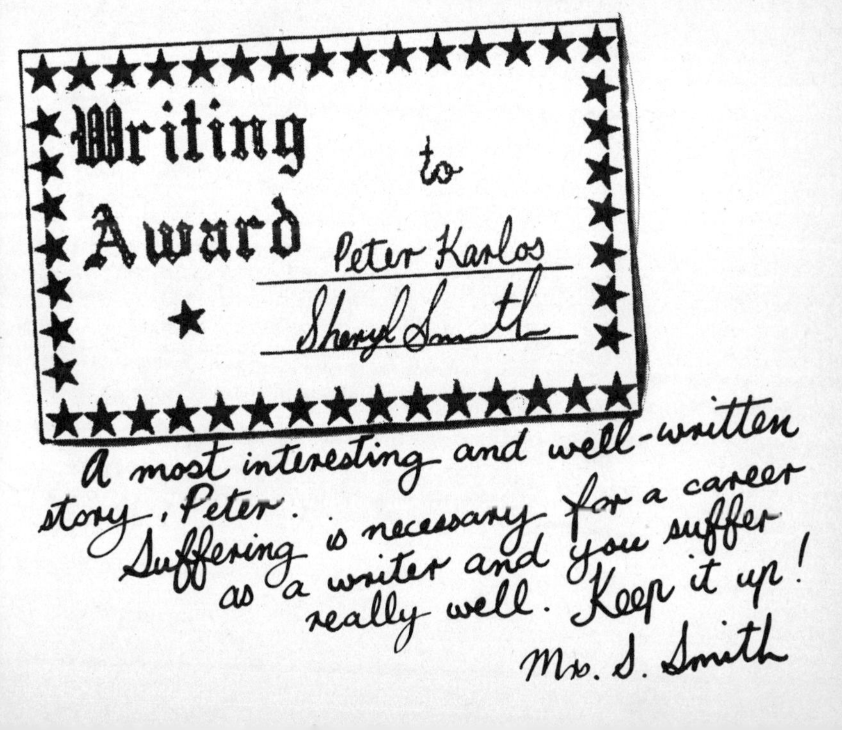

by Thadeus Antwerp

I have been studying Mrs Smith's methods of controlling naughty students, in particular Sam, Mario, Johnno and Jeremy Skinner. Unlike Mr Zeiner, whose class we can hear through the wall at all times, and Mr Bollie, whose voice we can hear from the oval most mornings, Mrs Smith keeps control merely by sliding her eyeballs sideways and piercing the victim with THE LOOK.

I use the word 'victim' because THE LOOK has more effect than threatening, shouting or detention. The victim usually becomes confused, blood rushes to his face, he breaks into a sweat, then the blood drains away, he becomes cold and begins to tremble. Mrs Smith then goes on with whatever she was doing and doesn't say a word.

Luckily she has never had to use this method on me as I am a very co-operative student. But some people, like those I mentioned earlier, seem to be unable to control themselves at times. I even saw her use it on Mr Monroe during sport one Friday afternoon.

It is rather pleasant in class when everyone is quietly working. Mrs Smith sits at her desk correcting work and occasionally slides her eyes around the room. We can hear the clock ticking, the phone in the office, Mr Bollie on the oval, and Mr Zeiner's class through the wall. When we finish our work we are free to read. I have already read two hundred and sixteen books this year and it is still only May. I aim to break the record of four hundred and one books, set ten years ago.

However I do worry that if my young cousin Basil were ever the victim of THE LOOK then it may kill him, as he has such a weak constitution and only a small amount of blood.

Me at footy with Mr B.

CooL Mr BoLLie

by Sam Lancer

Wednesday is the best day at school because we have Phys. Ed. with Mr Bollie.

He is a really great teacher. He even comes out at lunchtime and plays footy with us.

He is really cool. He wears shorts and a T-shirt even when it's cold, and most days he wears mirror shades. I'm going to get some of those.

So far this year we have learnt Hockey, Soccer, Lacrosse, Gymnastics and Newcombe.

Phys. Ed. is easy. I'm the best at it out of my grade. I've been captain four times already this year. The captain has got to keep his team in order. That's why some kids never get to be captain, because they can't keep me in order.

Mr Bollie has put me in charge of the equipment. I have to get two kids to help me get it out and put it away. I usually get Mario and Johnno to help, but not always. One day I got Thadeus and I made him take the Newcombe set down by himself. He is so hopeless.

I think we should have Phys. Ed. with Mr Bollie every day and only have Mrs Smith for an hour on Wednesdays.

Continuous Cricket

by Kirsty Dean

Who wants to play cricket? Not me. Bridgette doesn't want to either. Anyway, who ever heard of playing cricket in June?

Our school got a Phys. Ed. teacher this year. His name is Mr Bollie. We think his first name is Billy. Sometimes he and Mr Woodroff play footy at lunchtime, and they don't let the boys have a kick.

We have Phys. Ed. every Wednesday. Mr Bollie only likes kids who are good at sport, and girls who wear sports skirts. He doesn't like me. I'm not going to wear an awful brown sports skirt, or a brown track-suit. I never wear brown.

There's nothing wrong with what I wear. I have a very elegant purple and pink striped leotard which I co-ordinate with crimson tights and a crimson headband. If it's cold then I add my ballerina wrap. There's nothing wrong with trying to look good. Brown just doesn't go with my colouring.

Mr Bollie wears shorts that are too small and a T-shirt with the sleeves cut off. He just wants us to admire his muscles. Personally I find muscly men hideous. So does Bridgette.

This Wednesday, we had to play continuous cricket. We had two teams and the other team got to bat first. Our team had to stand out in the freezing cold wind, fielding. Mr Bollie ought to know that wind is bad for your skin. I stood with my back to it in order to protect my face. But I couldn't see the batter from that position so people kept yelling at me when the ball came near me. I didn't get to bowl because

Sam Lancer was captain again, and he only lets other boys bowl, but not Thadeus.

I only touched the ball twice and Bridgette didn't touch it at all.

We got the other team out for forty-seven runs. Then it was our turn to bat. We all lined up, but as usual, the boys, and Josephine Wood, pushed in at the front. I was eleventh and Bridgette was twelfth.

Just when it was my turn to bat, Mr Bollie blew the whistle for the end of the game. The score was forty-seven all. He said we'd run out of time, but we hadn't. He just wanted us to come a draw so people wouldn't fight. It wasn't playtime yet and Mrs Smith hates us coming back early.

Continuous cricket is stupid. So is Mr Bollie.

Bridgette thinks so too.

by Martin Peters

At lunchtime yesterday, Jeremy, David J and I went to the hall because Mr Zeiner was holding auditions for the school play. It's going to be a musical so he wanted to hear people sing.

Of course we weren't there to sing. We only came in because it was raining. We sat down the back near the heater with our feet up.

First Mr Z wanted to see how well some kids could skate and sing at the same time, because the play has seven roller-skating clones in it. Nobody could do it but he wrote down ten names anyway and said they had a week to practise, then he would see them again. The best seven would be in it, and the other three could be emergencies.

Then Mr Z said, 'Right, who wants to be Princess Confetti?'

All these girls jumped up saying, 'Me! Me!' and poor Mr Z had to stand on the piano-stool to get away from them. He said he wouldn't come down until they behaved like ladies. Then they took it in turns to sing. It was really funny. They all sang Kylie Minogue songs except for Kirsty Dean, who sang 'Vogue' just like Madonna. It was so funny that Jeremy stood up and did all the actions along with her.

That's when Mr Z noticed us and wanted to know if we were there to audition for the part of Prince Bruce, the space-ace hero. He said that seeing as Jeremy had some talent then he could go first.

'What can you sing?' asked Mr Z.

'Nothing,' said Jeremy.

'Try "Happy Birthday",' said Mr Z, and he started to play it on the piano.

So Jeremy tried 'Happy Birthday' but he forgot the words halfway through.

'You're the best we've got so far,' said Mr Z. 'You're next, Martin.'

But I'm not that silly. 'I've only come to audition to be a stage-hand,' I said.

'Me too,' said David.

'I see,' said Mr Z.

That's when Kirsty stood up and said that if HE (pointing to Jeremy) was going to be Prince Bruce, then she wouldn't go in the play at all and her mother wouldn't help with anything.

'I see,' said Mr Z. 'Sorry Jeremy, looks like you're a stage-hand as well.'

So Kirsty got the part of Princess Confetti and she gave Mr Z a list of boys whom she thought would be all right as Prince Bruce, but my name wasn't on it, thank goodness. And that's why SEARCHING FOR PRINCE BRUCE signs have gone up around the school.

SEARCHING FOR PRINCE BRUCE

Princess Confetti and Mr Zeiner are going to get You!

A Total Idiot

by Kathryn Chambers

There's a trench at the back of the new art room. It's very muddy. All the naughty little kids play a game called Cross-over, where they dare each other to jump the trench at the widest, deepest and muddiest places. They're not allowed to do this but they do it anyway. Someone acts as look-out to see if there's a teacher coming.

On Monday, when Joan and I were helping Miss Finly do yard-duty, we found Lorrie Lancer, a total idiot (inherited from his brother), with both his feet bogged in the trench. Miss Finly had to pull him out, but his shoes were left buried in the mud.

Lorrie complained about losing his shoes. He complained about having mud up to his knees. His socks were hanging off and his knees had gone blue with the cold.

Miss Finly said that if his shoes hadn't come off then his arms would have. She said he was lucky that he still had his legs and he'd better go to the office to explain why he'd been playing near the trench in the first place. He didn't want to go, so Joan and I had to take him. That's what Miss Finly asked us to do.

Lorrie didn't want to come with us so we had to hold on to his jumper. He really is disgusting. He always has his fly undone. Poor Miss Finly has to put up with him in her class every day.

Do you know what he told Mr Graves? He said that he just happened to be walking along when a strong gust of wind blew him sideways, he slipped on a wet rock, lost his balance and fell into the trench.

He is such a liar (just like his brother). Do you know what else he said? He said that his shoes were new and had cost fifty dollars, and could the school buy him a new pair.

And do you know what? The school *did* buy him a new pair. Can you believe that?

We're not going to help Miss Finly do yard-duty any more. Boys like Lorrie are really more closely related to chimpanzees than to us and shouldn't be considered part of the human race.

The history of the World

by Joan Smith

We all have to do a lecturette this term. That is when you have to stand out the front and talk about something for fifteen minutes. Then people can ask you questions, and you ask them questions and give out prizes if they get the answers right. Then Mrs Smith gives you a mark: A,B,C or D.

So far we have had four.

Josephine did hers on people who have won gold medals in the Olympic Games, and got a B. She even included the year 2000 and said she would win three that year but she hadn't decided which events she would go in yet. Sam Lancer said she would probably be in mud-wrestling, cow-pat-throwing and boy-kicking.

Josephine kicked him later on.

Martin Peters did his on how to keep blue-tongue lizards. He explained how he and his brother collected snails when it was raining and kept them in the freezer to feed to the lizards, and how his mother thought they were mini dim sims and put some in the steamer one day and cooked them for tea. Mrs Smith said they were probably better for you than dim sims and gave him a C.

Giant prehistoric Dinosnail

Jeremy Skinner did his on Australian food and gave us all Minties. Mrs Smith gave him a B. She was just being nice to him because he gave her his lamington sample. I don't think she should have eaten it because he had been holding it in his bare hands for ten minutes. Besides, if there was nothing wrong with it he would have eaten it himself.

Thadeus did his today. It was about the history of the world. He had a big ball of wool and he stapled the end of it to the middle of the blackboard ledge and wrote THE BEGINNING. Then he walked around and around the room, stapling the wool to the wall as he went. Every time he took a step he counted fifty-million years. Sometimes he would stop and say something like, 'This is when dinosaurs appeared on Earth,' and he would have a little piece of paper stuck to the wool with DINOSAURS APPEAR, TWO HUNDRED AND FIFTEEN MILLION YEARS AGO, written on it. Then he would give us a very long explanation of what the world was like at that time.

He walked around the room five times and the wool was stapled around the room five times. Eventually he came to the end of the wool, and on the last six centimetres there was a note saying HUMANS INHABIT EARTH.

His lecturette took two whole hours and Mrs Smith gave him AA++.

He only stopped long enough for us to go out to play, except some people didn't go out because they were asleep.

Kathryn's going to do hers on mutations. She says that girls are true human beings and boys are just mutations of girls.

I hate goody-goodies

by Sam Lancer

Goody-goodies are kids who are always good when teachers are watching, like Kathryn Chambers. But when teachers are not looking they are just as bad as everyone else, like Peter Karlos.

Goody-goodies are kids who spend ages colouring in their headings, like Joan Smith. But they still write notes and never sign them, like Kirsty Dean, and send them to kids they don't like.

Goody-goodies are kids who get A for everything whether it's good or not, like Thadeus Antwerp.

PRE-CAMBRIAN ERAS

Scale : 33⅓ (a) Scale : 2000/1 (b) Scale : 2/3 (c)

The Pre-Cambrian era was the time of simple forms of life: (a) an Amoeba, (b) a Flagellate, (c) Worms

EARTH FORMED 3,000–4,000 MILLION YEARS AGO (d) Thadeus Antwerp

You should have seen his lecturette. It was so stupid. All he did was walk around and around the room stapling wool to the wall, and counting backwards by millions.

He thought it was interesting telling us about jellyfish that lived zillions of years ago. Who cares? They're all dead now.

He thought it was just amazing when old-fashioned frogs crawled out of the slush squillions of years ago. No one else did. We all went to sleep.

We didn't wake up till the bell rang for hometime, and then we couldn't get through the door because of all the wool going across it.

I bet if I walked around the room stapling wool to the wall, Mrs Smith would give me EE--, and a detention.

My lecturette is going to be called 'I hate goody-goodies'.

by Kerrie Street

You would never believe it, but Mrs Smith has taught Nancy Cleary to read. No other teacher has been able to. Mrs Smith gives her special lessons every second day. Nobody thought it would ever work but it has. You'll never guess how we found out.

Today, Nancy put her hand up. Everyone was amazed because she has never put it up before. We all sat really quietly to hear what she would say.

Mrs Smith smiled at her and said, 'Yes, Nancy?'

'I found an exercise book,' said Nancy. 'And I don't know whose it is.'

'What name does it have on the cover?' asked Mrs Smith.

'It just says "The Lovers' Club",' said Nancy.

We all looked at each other, except some people who looked at the floor.

'Maybe there's something on the inside,' said Mrs Smith.

Nancy opened the book and began to read. 'Members,' she said. 'President, David Pierce' (we all looked at him but he only looked at Thadeus); 'Treasurer, David Smith' (he had his hands over his face); 'Secretary, Karl Dreschler' (he was under his desk pretending to look for his pen); 'Information Officer, Martin Peters' (he stood up and bowed); 'Personnel Manager, Ross Jenkins' (he just sat there looking at his fingernails).

'Very well read,' said Mrs Smith. 'Go on.'

'Employees,' went on Nancy. 'Poetry Writer, Thadeus Antwerp, fifty-cents per poem and thirty-cents per love-letter. Possible girlfriends: Mary Singer, 10/10; Kerrie Street, 8/10; Sally McKensie, 7/10; Bridgette O'Riley, 6/10 and Kirsty Dean, 5/10.'

Just as Nancy finished reading Kirsty's score, Kirsty stood up, put her hands on her hips and demanded to know how come she only got 5/10 and who was Mary Singer anyway, but Mrs Smith told her to sit down and be quiet, and asked Nancy if there was any more.

'Secrets,' read out Nancy.

'Right,' said Mrs Smith. 'I'll have that now, thank you. Isn't it marvellous, everyone, how well Nancy can read? I think she deserves a clap.'

So we all clapped and Nancy smiled and then we had to get on with our work.

I wonder what I got 8/10 for? I know who Mary Singer is. She lives round the corner from me, next door to David P, and has three little sisters. They all wear plaits and straw hats and go to St Mary's.

Factor X

by David Pierce

I'm in real trouble now. Nancy Cleary found our LOVERS' CLUB book and read it out to the whole class.

Mrs Smith said that because I was President then she was holding me responsible. That's not fair though, because all I do is say whose turn it is to speak at the meetings. I don't even do that much anyway, because Martin is the only one who ever says anything. Anyway, it was Martin who lost the book, so Mrs Smith ought to blame him. I do.

Mrs Smith wants to know on what basis we gave the girls a score out of ten. She said that for maths tomorrow she might let the girls score us, so that we could all learn about negative numbers. Anyway, Thads worked it out mathematically, and Mrs Smith probably wouldn't understand the formula. I didn't.

I added three points to Mary's score because I like her. Thads wrote this down as 'Factor X'. Now everyone wants to know who Mary is and how come she got 10/10, but I'm not telling them.

It's lucky Nancy didn't read out the bit about secrets, because then everyone would know lots of things, and David Smith would never come to school again. Mrs Smith said she might read out that bit herself tomorrow, depending on whether or not we give her a headache today.

Questionnaire

LOVERS' CLUB

President David Pierce Secretary Karl Dreschler

Questionnaire

1. What sport do you like most?
   A. Football
   B. Soccer
   C. Netball
   D. Other

2. Who do you barrack for?
   A. Bulldogs
   B. Tigers
   C. Eagles
   D. Magpies
   E. Bears
   F. Swans
   G. Blues
   H. Other

3. What is your favourite TV program?
   ....

4. Do you have your own cassette-player?
   ....

5. Do you like food from around the world?
   ....

6. What is your eye colour?
   ....

7. What is your hair colour?
   ....

8. What id your favourite comic-book person?
   ....

9. Do you have? (please tick)
   A. Pet
   B. Bike
   C. Skateboard
   D. Roller Skates
   E. Computer
   F. Other

10. Can you swim without touching the bottom?
   .... P.T.O

Now that everyone knows about the club, lots of people want to join. They will have to pay two dollars and Thads is going to get them to fill in a questionnaire, and then he's going to put all the information into his computer-matching program. The only problem is, the program can't cope with Factor X. All the program wants to know is what your interests are and what colour eyes and hair you like. If Mary gets matched up with anyone else, then I'm going to resign from the Presidency. I wonder if President Bush gets the blame for everything?

KOALA HILLS PRIMARY SCHOOL

Newsletter no. 20   23rd June

From Mr Graves, Principal

Well, I expect we all need and deserve a holiday and let's hope the weather improves and the mud dries up before term three starts.

I am sorry to say that the new art room will not be completed in the near future as originally planned; in fact work has stopped completely for the time being due to a lack of funds and rising costs. May I suggest that parents contact their local Member of Parliament and put a little pressure on him on our behalf. Dad said he wouldn't even notice a sledgehammer on the head.

The New Art Room
Photographed
last week

HELP NEEDED

Mr Jergens is desperate. He needs assistants in the library to help with cataloguing, covering and shelving new books. If you can help, even for one morning per month, please let us know.

Dad is making a piece of sculpture in honour of Mr Jergens called 'Desperation'.

Mr Zeiner would like to hear from people who have a sewing machine and would be able to make costumes for the school production which will be a futuristic musical set in the 21st century. He particularly needs a galactic-princess costume, several cosmic villains, a chorus of universal troopers, seven roller-skating clones and a space-ace super-hero. *I am one of these. So is Kerrie Street.*

ADVERTISEMENTS

Mr Tom Johnson, of Tojo's Old and New Autos, can provide you with any model, any make, any time at any price. Drop in, at 3 Wattle Tree Rd, or enquire by phone. 729 02145

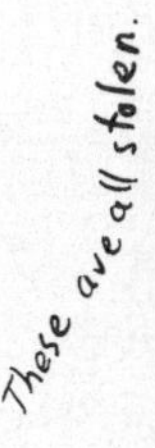

Are you being controlled by credit or bothered by bankers? Contact Mr P Antwerp and discuss how you too could be planning for profit. 732 68127

For one dollar, this space could be yours. Contact our advertising executive, Mrs Lawson, for advice and copy writing. Results guaranteed or your money refunded.

732 89105

MY HOLIDAY by Thadeus Antwerp

It was Mother's idea that during the term holidays, we should study some cultures other than our own.

'Melbourne,' she said, 'is home to people from all over the world, and one way to understand them is to eat their food.'

She didn't actually mean that we should go out and eat other people's food. She meant that we should go to a few different restaurants. We tried Chinese, Vietnamese, African, Italian, Greek and Turkish.

We didn't bother taking Basil because Mother said it's a waste

of money buying food for him, as he has such a sensitive stomach and an over-active immune system, which causes allergic reactions to almost everything. So Mother, Father and I usually went alone except for the Turkish restaurant where we met several of Father's colleagues.

The food was quite delectable, very plentiful and extremely cheap. We started with a variety of dips and mounds of flat bread. This was followed by salads and meat dishes, more bread, more food, more bread, and so on. While we kept eating, the food kept coming, the last plates being of Turkish sweets.

Father's colleagues are all rather like Father. The conversation went on and on, from the number of moons around Jupiter to the Greenhouse Effect, and then to their boss, who wasn't there.

They talked about him until the belly-dancer appeared.

BY THADEUS ANTWERP

How can I describe her?
She was a large woman with an enormous amount of exposed white flesh which quivered like jelly as she held her arms aloft and shook herself closer and closer to our table. There were fringes and beads which seemed to be alive, clinging to her hips as she tried to shake them off.

I wondered about which engineering principles were employed in the construction of the garment which held up her overflowing bosom, by now almost touching Father's eyeballs. What a fantastic anti-gravity device it must be.

I was just about to remark to Mother about these observations I had been making, when she said it was time to go home.

So we left.

Writing Award

to Thadeus Antwerp

Mrs S. Smith

A most perceptive and well-written account, Thadeus. Your use of language is excellent, however please note that this award is specifically for your writing and NOT for your drawing which I think illustrates your over-active imagination rather than your scientific observations.

Mrs S. Smith

THE WRONG LUNCH
by Martin Peters

A funny thing happened today. We were just about to have lunch when the door opened and a little prep kid came in. She skipped right up to Mrs Smith and said, 'Petsie's got the wrong lunch.'

Mrs Smith looked at her and said, 'Did you knock before coming in?'

The little kid held up a bag and said, 'This is Petsie's lunch and he's got mine.'

Mrs Smith looked at her even harder and said, 'I don't think I asked you to come in.'

The little kid skipped up to Peter Karlos and said, 'I don't like olive sandwiches, Petsie. I want my own lunch.'

Everyone laughed, except Peter and Mrs Smith.

Fancy having olive sandwiches.

Mrs Smith stood up and Petsie tried to sink down lower.

'Who is this child, Peter?' said Mrs Smith. 'She doesn't seem to have very good manners.'

Peter said it was his little sister, Sylvia, and that she was too little to have manners because she had only just turned five.

'Off you go then, Sylvia,' said Mrs Smith, and Sylvia skipped off, without closing the door behind her.

Fancy being called 'Petsie'. That's really funny.

by Peter Karlos

People are being awful to me.

They think I tell lies, even though I don't any more. When I brought my photo album with pictures of us at Disneyland, only Nancy Cleary believed they were real, and she doesn't count.

Sam practises head-locks and karate-chops on me.

Jeremy makes me have lunch-orders every Friday because he says he needs extra carbohydrates so he can play well on the footy team.

Yesterday Josephine Wood pushed me in the mud near the half-built art room, just because I said she was a girl. Kirsty and Bridgette helped me out of the mud and Kirsty said it was only because they hate Josephine more than they hate me.

Today my little sister Sylvia came in to swap lunches with me, because Mum had given us the wrong ones by mistake. I didn't really mind having hers. I would have eaten sugar sandwiches if I had to, rather than ask Mrs Smith if I could go and swap. But Sylvia doesn't mind asking anything and she actually came right into our room, without knocking, called me 'Petsie', and told everyone that she doesn't like olive sandwiches.

Now everyone calls me 'Petsie' just because they know I don't like it, and if I shout at them they call me 'Olive' instead.

I've tried really hard to be nice, but it doesn't work.

The only thing to do is to be awful back.

THE EXCURSION

By Martin Peters

I don't know why, but Mrs Smith has been teaching us about soap, so we got to go and visit a soap factory.

It really stank. It smelt like they were boiling up dead animals. Thadeus said they were, and all the girls said, 'Oh, yukky- poo!'

Then poor Petsie Karlos went green, fell on the floor and banged his head on the concrete.

Bridgette O'Riley said, 'Oh, he's dead!' and started screaming, and Jeremy said, 'Good!'

But Mrs Smith said, 'Come on Jeremy, you're a big strong chap, help me carry him out.'

So they carried him out to the tea-room.

Jeremy can't really be as strong as he reckons, because he dropped his end first (the head end) and Petsie banged his head on the floor again. This time Peter went grey and you can guess what he did. He did it all over Jeremy's legs and feet.

Mrs Smith said it served Jeremy right for dropping Peter's head. She made them both sit outside in the fresh air – Peter because he still felt sick and Jeremy because he smelt more awful than usual.

We all went through the soap factory without them, and when we got back, Jeremy had wiped his legs with Peter's hair.

Then Bridgette shouted at Jeremy and called him a fat fool with a face like a camel.

No one had ever heard Bridgette shout before. We were all amazed. Then she hit him on the head with her lunch-box and pushed him over.

Mario told on Bridgette to Mrs Smith, but all she said was that it would probably do Jeremy good and that Mario had better watch out because he might be next.

THE SOAP FACTORY

by Thadeus Antwerp

Mrs Smith has taken us to some very interesting places this year. I really must tell you about our visit to a soap factory.

Of course I knew that soap is made from animal fat, and so did Mrs Smith, but no one else in the class did. When it was explained, Peter declared that he would never wash again, and collapsed in a dead faint on the factory floor.

The smell was sickening – not of Peter, but of the fat. I could understand his revulsion, but mine was overshadowed by a scientific interest in the whole procedure – not only of the soap production, but of Peter's expiration.

It was interesting to watch the blood drain from his face and to see his complexion change from hot-pink to lettuce-green. It was remarkable how limp his arms and legs had become, and how his eyeballs had turned up towards his brain so that only white could be seen through slitted lids. It amazed me how quickly gravity had attracted his body to the floor once his brain had turned off, and what a loud noise his head made when it hit the concrete.

Mrs Smith and Jeremy Skinner had to carry poor Peter to the tea-room, where his recovery was aided by a handful of chocolate freckles. I felt it my duty to inform him that the very same thing that had offended him earlier was probably the main ingredient in chocolate.

Luckily he didn't faint again, but he did do something even more unpleasant, on Jeremy. They both had to sit outside in the fresh air while we continued our tour of the factory.

Jeremy wasn't pleased.

Rehearsals

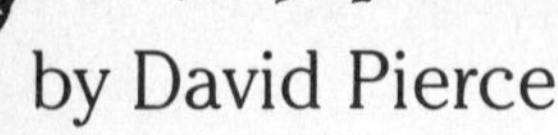

by David Pierce

We have rehearsals for the school play on Monday afternoons and Thursday mornings. That means we get out of doing WORK twice every week.

I have a part as a roller-skating clone. So has Kerrie and Josephine and four other kids. We have to skate in and out of the actors while the universal troopers sing.

In fact, singing is the only thing the troopers do. They are really the school choir, but when they were called 'the school choir' nobody would join. Now that they're called 'universal troopers' there are twenty-five of them.

Thadeus has to play his violin in the orchestra and Kirsty is Princess Confetti. She thinks she is THE STAR. Thads thinks she is THE STAR too. He keeps watching her instead of Mr Zeiner, who tries to conduct the orchestra.

Kirsty tried to get me to be Prince Bruce, but luckily I can't sing.

It took Mr Z eight weeks to find someone to be Prince Bruce and that was only because a new kid came into grade six and Mr Z got him to agree before he knew what he would have to do.

Kirsty's mother is supposed to be making us all costumes but she doesn't have time so us roller-skaters have to wear black clothes with strips of foil wrapped around our bodies. We have to cover our bike helmets with foil and stick silver pipe-cleaners on to them. We look like space bees.

All of the grade-two boys have parts as cosmic villains and they get to slash around with laser-swords painted fluorescent green. Mr Z usually sends them back to class early because they always manage to cause trouble.

Yesterday they had a fight with each other instead of with Prince Bruce, and Miss Martiner, the first-aid teacher, had to be sent for. It was a real massacre with only Lorrie Lancer left standing.

After the blood was cleaned up and all the villains were sent to either the sick-bay or the office, Thads went really pale because we couldn't find Basil anywhere. Mr Z said he might have slipped down a gap between the floorboards, but he was really only joking.

Eventually we found him when the curtain was drawn. He had been lost on the wrong side of it in amongst the folds and couldn't find his way out, so he said.

Rehearsals are really funny. They're much better than sitting in class doing WORK.

I Knew That

by Joan Smith

David Johnson can't do anything and doesn't know anything.

When Mrs Smith has just finished explaining something, like maths, he always says, 'I don't get it.'

So she has to explain it all over again, just for him, and he still doesn't get it. Then she has to sit down with him and help him do the first bit, and that's usually the only bit he gets right.

When Mrs Smith tells us what to do for homework, David never listens, and then he says, 'What do we have to do for homework?'

So she has to explain it all over again, but David never does his homework anyway.

Today, Mrs Smith explained all about our project. It took her ages, and when she had finished, David said, 'I don't get it.'

So she had to explain it all over again, but when she had finished this time, David said, 'I knew that.'

Then Mrs Smith turned around and banged her head three times on the blackboard.

I wanted to be **sure** I knew.

By Kerrie Street

Mr Bollie is a mean man. He is really awful. Do you know what he did?

We were doing Phys. Ed. in the hall because it was raining again. We were playing skittles. That's when each team has three wooden skittles, and everyone else has to be a human skittle, except for one person on each team who throws the ball. You're supposed to protect your wooden skittles with your body. If the ball hits you then you're out, but if you catch the ball then everyone on your team who is out can come back in.

This game gets a bit rough and some people throw the ball too hard. This is what happened today.

It was all right until Josephine Wood got to be ball-thrower at one end and Sam Lancer at the other. They both think that you have to throw the ball really hard at other people's heads.

Mr Bollie didn't even stop them because I don't think he can see properly with his sun-glasses on in the hall when it's raining and the lights are out.

Josephine hit Kirsty right on the nose. It bled all over her beautiful purple leotard and blood ran down her pink tights and dripped onto the carpet.

And do you know what Mr Bollie said? All he said was, 'Bleed in the bin, not on the floor.'

He's not very nice, is he?,

Drawing by Kerrie Street

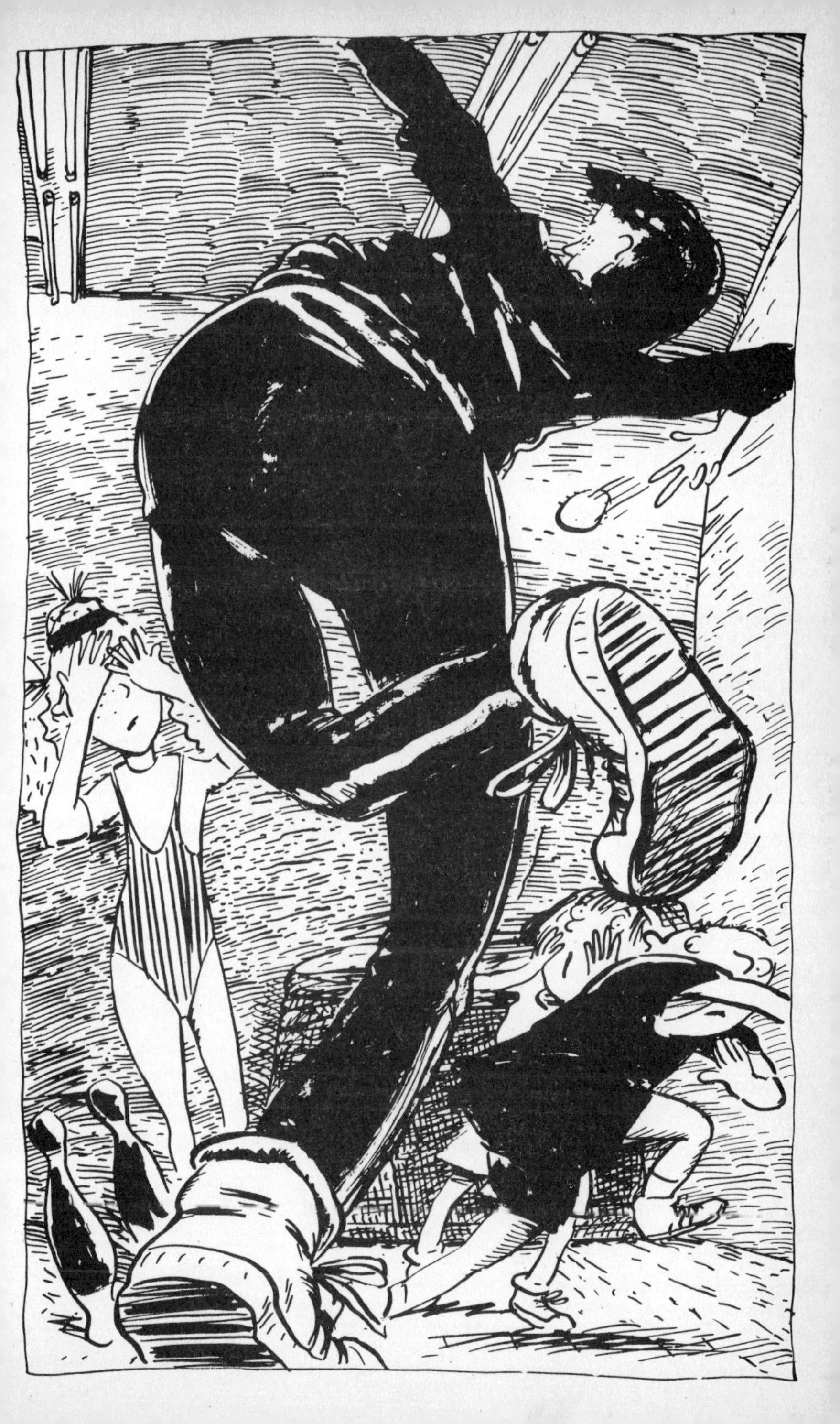

Getting Signatures

By Kathryn Chambers

Mrs Smith is quite good really. She gives us signatures for doing good work. On Thursday afternoons we can trade them in for free time.

Mrs Smith writes a list of things we can choose from on the blackboard, and if we have enough signatures then we can do them. People who don't have any have to do dictionary work.

Today she put up drawing, playing board-games, weeding the fern garden, playing computer-games, tidying the teacher's desk, helping Mr Jergens in the library and sweeping the gravel off the asphalt. Then we had to decide how many signatures each thing was worth. This depends on how many people want to do it.

Nearly everybody wanted to sweep the asphalt (not Joan or I though). So Mrs Smith auctioned it.

'Who wants to do it for five signatures?' she said. There were still six people but only three brooms.

'Six?' said Mrs Smith. There were still four people.

'Seven?'

Sam, Mario and Johnno paid seven signatures each to sweep the asphalt, and Mrs Smith let them outside to do it without watching them. It's no wonder they ended up at the office.

Joan and I tidied Mrs Smith's table. It was really messy. We put all the confiscated yo-yos and turtle cards in a plastic bag in the filing cabinet under 'J' for 'Junk'. It only cost us one signature each to do that job.

I've still got forty-three left and Joan has thirty-eight. Most people only get about five per week. I didn't think Sam Lancer had any. If I were the teacher he wouldn't have.

It's NOT FAIR

By Sam Lancer

Mrs Smith doesn't give David Johnson any signatures because she doesn't like him. She reckons she only gives them to kids for doing really good work, but she gave me one for my maths and half of it was wrong.

Half of David's was wrong too but she still didn't give him one. He got the same half wrong that I did. That was the half that he copied from me, that I had copied from Mario.

The half that I copied from Peter I got right. That's because David Smith helped him do it.

David Johnson copied that half straight from David Smith. So the half that David J got right is the same half that I got right.

I got a signature for mine, but David J didn't, and that's not fair.

Martin can do Mrs Smith's signatures really well. We all reckoned that it wasn't fair that David was the only person in the class who didn't have one, so Martin did one on the half of his maths that was right. Then lots of kids wanted them on their work, because you get to trade them in on Thursdays for free time. The more you've got then the more free time you can have. When you trade them in, Mrs Smith puts a circle around them so you can't use them again.

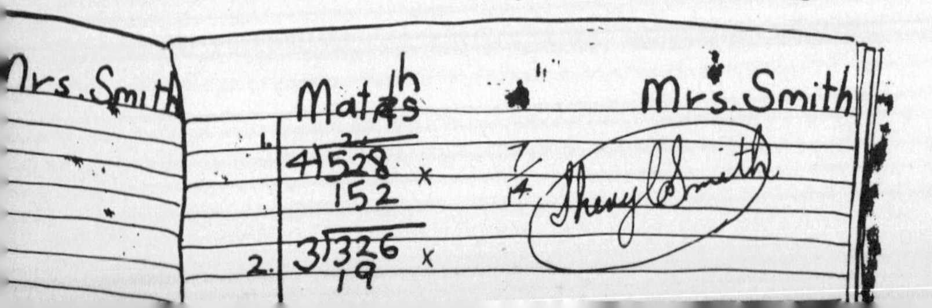

Today, Mario, Johnno and I used ours to have free time to sweep the asphalt. It was totally radical. We played Bridge Fights, Attack the School and Pole Vaulting.

Martin said that next week he's going to charge fifty-cents for each signature, but that's not fair because David J doesn't get any pocket-money. He told us his dad said that if he wants something then he'll just have to learn to steal it. But that's not fair either because you can't steal signatures.

This is my new way of drawing fa
Isn't it good.

by Kirsty Dean

I have a new boyfriend. His name is Jesse P Gillis. He is so gorgeous. He's from California and is in grade six. He had to kiss me in the school play during Act 4. It was the love scene.

No one else wanted to play the part of the space-ace because of the kiss but Jesse kissed me and now he's my boyfriend. Compared to him, all the other boys are just so childish.

The play was really good. I was the star. I played Princess Confetti, who went on a quest to find the lost key of the ancient dome of Vulcania. On the way I met the space-ace hero, Prince Bruce, who was played by Jesse. He is just so gorgeous.

My mum made all the costumes for the play, even Mr Zeiner's purple cloak and hat. My dress was really beautiful. It was the best costume of all. It had lots of frilly bits and shiny beads sewn all over the front. It took Mum thirty-six hours to make it.

I don't want David Pierce for my boyfriend any more, so I'm going to let Bridgette have him. That means she won't need David Smith from now on, so we're going to give him to Kerrie.

Poor Bridgette had to sit next to Peter Karlos to play their flutes in the orchestra for the play. Nobody would want Peter for their boyfriend, so we're letting Nancy Cleary have him.

At the end of the play, Princess Confetti and Prince Bruce (Jesse and I) had to sing a song together. Jesse looks just like Jordan Knight (well almost) and can sing like him as well. He is so gorgeous. Bridgette thinks so too.

Just after we finished our song, I was attacked by a cosmic villain. It was really Lorrie Lancer. I don't think Mr Zeiner should have let the grade-two boys be in the play. I think he only did it because Miss Finly couldn't stand them being in her grade any more, and wanted to get rid of them every afternoon for rehearsals. I think they should all be expelled, especially L Lancer (and his brother).

Now, just because my head is bandaged up, everyone is saying that all my hair was cut off before the stitches were put in, but it's not true. Anyway, my mum has some special ointment to make hair grow back quicker.

THE SCHOOL PLAY

by Thadeus Antwerp

Unfortunately, Mr Zeiner wrote all the music for the school play. I suppose that if he were any good at song-writing then he wouldn't be a teacher.

Most of the music was suitable for electric guitars and drums, neither of which we have in the orchestra. I found it rather difficult to pick out a melody appropriate for a violin.

Unfortunately, Mr Zeiner wrote, produced and directed the whole play, and conducted the orchestra, for which he wore an alarming purple cloak. I really don't think his talents lie in this field.

Mr Zeiner and Kirsty Dean (I really think he has a Napoleonic complex)

My poor little cousin Basil was cast as a cosmic villain, along with most of the other boys in his class. He was required to fight with a laser-sword, an activity completely against his peaceful nature. I'm afraid he crumpled under the weight of his costume early in Act 2, and no one noticed until Act 5, when he was found lying at the back of the stage, unable to get up without assistance.

Luckily, Mr Zeiner had nothing to do with the costumes, and they were wonderful. Kirsty looked very pretty as Princess Confetti, but I don't think Jesse Gillis was a suitable hero, looking rather more like a Hittite than a Homosapien. I actually would have liked that part myself, and would have auditioned for it if I hadn't been needed for the orchestra.

I certainly wouldn't be put off by a kiss as all the other boys were. After all, it was only a kiss on the hand, and Princess Confetti was wearing gloves, and the space-ace was wearing a mask. He couldn't possibly have caught anything.

I do think that fifteen cosmic villains was too many, especially as they were armed with green sticks. When Kirsty was assaulted during the finale, I would have been the first to her side if I hadn't still been required by the orchestra. As they say, the show must always go on.

She was driven to the hospital in full costume, and all she missed was the party for the cast. This wasn't really worth going to as Basil wasn't catered for. There was no distilled water provided and he just can't digest party food. I felt it would be rude to eat in front of him.

I noticed that Jesse P Gillis enjoyed himself, but I fear he may be addicted to Coca-Cola.

KOALA HILLS PRIMARY SCHOOL

Newsletter no. 29 22nd September

From Mr Graves, Principal

Congratulations, Mr Zeiner, and well done. What a great effort you and your fellow Thespians have made. I must in particular mention our galactic princess, Kirsty Dean, of grade five, who stole the show with her amazing costume and beautiful singing.

It was unfortunate (and not in the script) that Kirsty was attacked during the last act by one of our over-enthusiastic cosmic villains. We have been assured that there is no permanent damage and that the stitches should be out before next term commences.

Thanks must go to our resident seamstress, Mrs Dean, who was responsible for all the costumes.

Ticket sales raised a total of $327.91, which will be added to the 'finish the art room' fund. Only $24,678.00 to go to cover the shortfall between funding provided by the government, and the amount required by the builders before they come back to work. If anyone has any ideas as to how we can raise this amount, please let us know.

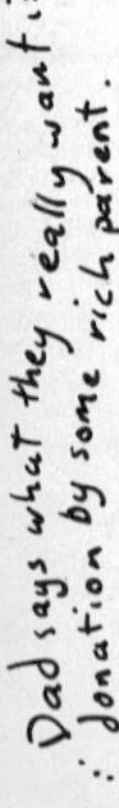

HELP NEEDED

I am sorry to say that due to ill health, Mr Jergens will be on leave all next term. He is being replaced by his wife, Mrs Jergens. If anyone is able to help her with a backlog of covering, cataloguing and shelving books, we would love to see you in the library any time any day.

The fete committee needs volunteers to staff the stalls at our grand fete, to be held on November 10th. Please contact our fete co-ordinator, Mrs Lawson. 732 89105

The Parents Club intends to publish a recipe book entitled *Recession Recipes*. They are currently looking for contributions which would 'feed a family of four for five dollars'. Please leave your suggestions with the convenor of our Parents Club, Mrs Lawson, in the general office.

Mum's going to donate a recipe made from eggs and silver beat. I don't recommend it!

ADVERTISEMENTS

Mr Tom Johnson, of Tojo's Personalised Autos, can get any addition to any model any time, cheap. Phone for an appointment. He's going to steal them. 729 02145

Mrs Dean, of 3 Pleasant Cres, provides a dressmaking service, second to none which caters for all. Fantasy dressing a specialty. 756 90324

Are you being destroyed by your debts, mauled by your mortgage and berated by your bankers? Phone Mr P Antwerp for friendly financial advice. 732 68127

Dad says he's being destroyed by his diet of eggs and silver beat. Yuk.

Advertisements can be prepared for you by Mrs H Lawson. Reasonable rates. Ph. Koala Hills P.S. 732 89105

My Cousin Cristobelle

by Kirsty Dean

I'm glad Cristobelle has gone home at last. I don't think she's beautiful at all. She has pimples and tells lies. She said that she had a real boyfriend. I bet she hasn't.

I had been looking forward to her coming, because it gets a bit boring during the holidays, but after three days I was sick of her.

When she arrived she had a large suitcase full of clothes and jewellery, and another case full of make-up and nail polish. We went to my room straight away so that she could show me all her things.

Cristobelle gave me one of her passport photos.

Isn't she a showoff!

I don't even have a passport.

I think I hate her!

I had to let her sleep in my bed with my white lace quilt cover, and I slept on a mattress on the floor with two ancient grey blankets. Cristobelle hung all her clothes in my wardrobe, and squashed mine up one end.

When we were lying in bed that night, she told me all about her boyfriend. His name is Pino. She went on and on about him. He has a skateboard with a skull on it, and a job delivering newspapers. He wears black jeans and has curly hair. He's really lovely, so she thinks!

The next morning Cristobelle arranged all her things on my dressing-table, and pushed my things to the back. Then she showed me how to put on make-up.

She said she could make my fat cheeks look slimmer by shading them with eye-shadow. She said that she knew a lady who had a nose like mine who had to have plastic surgery to fix it.

Mummy took this photo of Me and Cristobelle. She says I don't have fat cheeks and my nose is pretty.

Then she did my hair, but first there were a few pieces sticking out that needed trimming. She said she knew all about hairdressing because her friend Tiffany was going to be a hairdresser.

We went outside and I stood very still while she styled my hair with her nail scissors. There seemed to be a lot on the ground.

Cristobelle said that pink and purple were out this year and that black, green and orange were in. She put all of my pink and purple clothes in the bottom drawer and said not to wear them or I'd be a dag. She said that socks had to be folded down this year and not rolled, and that I ought to have a pair of bicycle shorts even though I don't have a bicycle. I didn't have anything left to wear so Cristobelle lent me some of her clothes. They were a bit big and I didn't really like them, but I thought I better wear them anyway. I don't think orange is my colour.

That night Cristobelle went on and on about Pino again. He's in Year 8 and she lets him kiss her at the back of the oval at lunch-time. He's going to be a rock star and even has his own band called Concrete Bronze. So she says!

The next day we went swimming. Cristobelle wore an orange and green bikini and actually tried to get a suntan, even though it was only September. She'll get awful freckles and wrinkles. I kept my hat and shirt on and stayed in the shade even though she said I was a dag.

Some boys came and hung around her. They pushed each other and did silly jumps into the deep end of the pool. Cristobelle thought they were funny. I just wanted to go home.

That night she went on and on about Pino again. He has a lovely smile and walks home with her on Tuesdays because he has guitar lessons at her neighbour's place. She said that I'd know how she felt about Pino in three years time when I was mature like her. So I told her about my boyfriend Jesse, but she just laughed and said he wasn't a real boyfriend like Pino. I was getting sick of Cristobelle and Pino.

The next day I invited Bridgette around. We were going to do some embroidery. Cristobelle was outside sunbaking and reading a book called 'Lost Love on a Tropical Island'. I introduced them. Cristobelle looked at Bridgette for a few minutes and said that she could give her a make-over if she liked. Bridgette looked at me and I said 'No thanks' for her. We went inside and left Cristobelle to go wrinkly in the sun.

After Bridgette left, Cristobelle said what a dag she was and that I'd never be 'in' until I found a new friend.

Cristobelle isn't very nice. I don't like her at all. I had to put up with her for eleven more days. She's not even beautiful. I bet Pino doesn't even exist. It'll take two months to grow my hair back. Purple and pink are lovely colours.

I am not a dag. Bridgette doesn't think I am either.

Writing Award

to Kirsty Dean

Mrs S. Smith

Well done, Kirsty. Right from the heart – that's the way to write.

Cristobelle does sound like a pain. She reminds me of someone in this class. Can you guess who?

Mrs. S. Smith

THE HIT LIST

by Kerrie Street

Our poor art teacher, Miss Martiner, is going off her brain. Do you want to know why?

Partly it is because they haven't finished building the new art room, and they are not going to because the school has run out of money. Miss Martiner has to teach in the corridor because there are too many things in her room, like boards and old sinks.

Partly it's because there are only scraps left to do art with because Miss Martiner won't buy anything new until she has a store-room to lock everything in, otherwise kids will steal stuff. So will teachers probably.

But mainly she's going mad because most kids think that art isn't really work, so they mess about. They do the stupidest things.

Take Mario Marati for instance. We were doing sewing last week and he sewed all his fingers together. Then he walked around saying, 'Ahh, ahh, I've got stitches.' Miss Martiner said he would have real stitches soon.

And you wouldn't believe this, but some girls put glue all over their hands so that they can peel it off later.

The stupidest thing of all was when David Johnson pulled the toes of his socks out from the holes in his shoes, and cut them off.

Miss Martiner said that that was the last straw. She said that from now on she wouldn't put up with any ratbaggery and that anyone who was on her hit list could clean the trough with a toothbrush next week.

She said that her hit list was a list of people who needed hitting, but as she wasn't allowed to hit them then she would make them do something really boring, like picking all the staples out of the wall, or counting the toothpicks, or scraping the clay off the floor, or sharpening the crayons.

When she mentioned sharpening the crayons, David Johnson said, 'Can I do that? It would be more fun than making things out of scraps.'

But Miss Martiner didn't say anything.
She just went sort of purplish.

The School Fete

by David Pierce

The school fete was really good. I went with my girlfriend, Mary, and her little sister, Alice, and her littler sister, Victoria. We met Thadeus and his cousin Basil there. Thads said that he had to look after Basil all day, because both their mothers were running the frozen lasagne stall, and both their fathers were manning the car-wash. We said we didn't mind as we had to look after Mary's little sisters as well.

Mary and her sisters looked pretty good. They were wearing the right sort of clothes. So was I, and Thadeus almost was except for the towelling hat. Basil's legs are so thin that his bike shorts flapped around them like flags, and his T-shirt was so long that some of it was hanging out the bottom of his shorts.

Mary and I walked around together, and Thads and Alice sort of almost walked around together, but not quite, and

Basil and Victoria followed us. First we all had a go on the 'throw the coin in the square' game. Basil won two dollars and we got him to buy us some fairy-floss. He didn't eat any himself though because he's allergic to pink colouring and sugar.

Then we all had a go on the jumping castle, except Basil, who gets motion sickness very easily. After that we went to the white-elephant stall and Thads bought twenty books. He said they were all his own really, because his mother had donated them to the stall. We had to help him carry them around for the rest of the day.

Then we went to play the video-games. Mary and I were having a great time, but the flashing lights made Basil dizzy and he had to be helped outside. While he was resting, Lorrie Lancer appeared from nowhere with three of his lunatic friends and challenged Basil to a fight. Basil was still feeling faint, so Mary's little sister Victoria stood in a karate position, screamed really loudly and stamped on Lorrie's toe. While he was hopping up and down, she pushed him over and his three friends sort of backed away and just left him there. So we won.

We walked all the way around the fete again and spent the rest of our money, then left all our stuff with Mrs Antwerp while we played gang tiggy with some other kids: Martin, David S, Peter, Sylvia, Kerrie, Sally, Bridgette and Kirsty.

Actually, Basil didn't play. He lay down in the shade and had a rest.

When we got home, Mary said that she still thinks Thadeus is weird, but Basil is weirder.

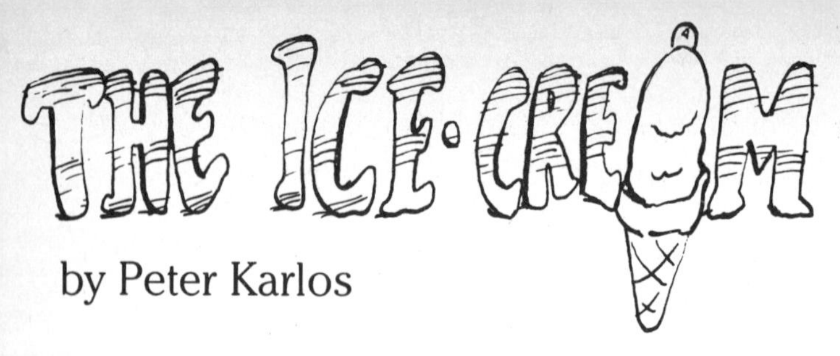

by Peter Karlos

I went to the school fete today. I had to mind my little sister Sylvia. She thought I had to hold her hand all day as well. Mum was helping on the jam and chutney stall and Dad was at work.

Sylvia starts every sentence with 'I want'. She dragged me all over the place and made me buy her stuff. If I don't then she runs to Mum and cries and carries on and then Mum shouts at me.

At the fete I saw Thadeus minding his cousin Basil, Kathryn Chambers minding her little brother Hugh, and Josephine Wood minding her little brother, the twins and a kid in a pusher. That was really funny seeing Josephine with these little kids all asking for stuff at the same time and trying to get away from her. She even had two of them on leads like dogs. She made a face at me.

I also saw Kirsty Dean hanging around with that American kid, Jesse Gillis. She poked her tongue out at me.

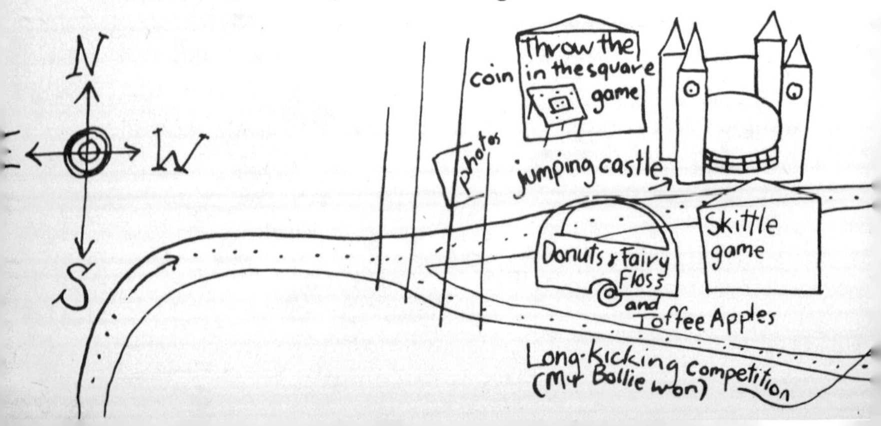

Then I saw Bridgette O'Riley sitting by herself. She smiled at me and said 'Hello' to Sylvia. Sylvia sat next to her, so I had to sit down as well. I had almost thought of something to say when Sylvia said, 'Petsie, I want an ice-cream.'

Bridgette didn't even say anything about her calling me Petsie. Anyone else would have.

I gave Sylvia both ice-creams to hold while I paid for them and she gave mine to Bridgette and said, 'Petsie bought this one for you.'

I was almost going to say something, but instead I went back and bought another one for myself. After that I couldn't get rid of Bridgette. I didn't really want to anyway. She came all around with us and Sylvia held on to her hand instead of mine. When we went past Kirsty (Jesse had gone), Bridgette pretended she didn't see her. Kirsty made a face at me.

After a while we played gang tiggy with everyone else, except that Bridgette and Sylvia and I were the hardest to find because we hid in the same place together.

I was almost going to say something to Bridgette before we went home, but I didn't have to because Sylvia talked all the time. It was lucky I had to mind her. I had a good time at the school fete.

Playing Madball

by Kirsty Dean

Miss Crumble is our student teacher. We're having her for six weeks. We think her name is Violette. She is beautiful. She is almost as beautiful as I am going to be when I'm grown up.

She wears lovely clothes, although I think she should throw out all the grey ones and wear crimson instead.

She has an engagement ring with a huge ruby in it. It really is nice, but I would prefer a diamond.

Miss Crumble has been coming with us to Phys. Ed. so that she can learn how to teach it. Since she has been coming, Mr Bollie has been wearing clean socks and has washed his shoes.

Today he had even polished his muscles. All he did was sit on the seat in the sun with his sun-glasses on while Miss Crumble took us.

She's really good. She let Thadeus and I be captains. He had Kerrie on his team to tell him what to do, and I had David P on my team, and I asked him what to do.

We played Madball. One team has to take it in turns to hit the ball with a tennis racquet. The other team has to get the ball and throw it to each other until they have all had a turn at throwing and catching. While they do that, the person who hit the ball makes runs. It's a good game because you can't go out and it doesn't matter if you drop the ball.

Everyone who was rude got sent off to sit next to Mr Bollie. After about ten minutes there were only fourteen of us left playing and I got to touch the ball twenty-five times.

I wish we had Miss Crumble for Phys. Ed. all the time.

There's no point in Mr Bollie trying to impress her with his muscles and his tan, because she already has a boyfriend, and we told him so.

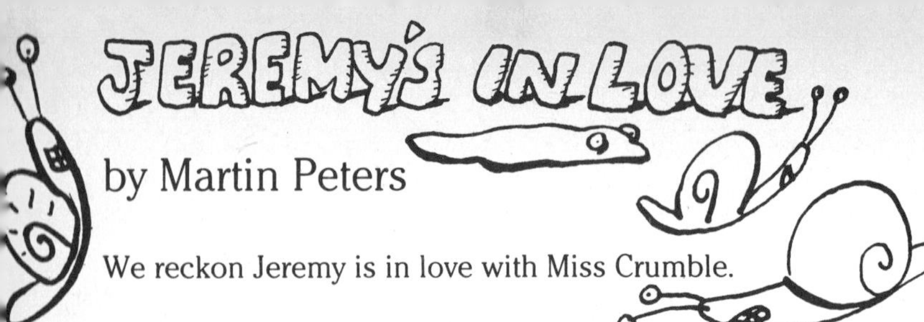

JEREMY'S IN LOVE

by Martin Peters

We reckon Jeremy is in love with Miss Crumble.

Lots of people think you can be naughty for student teachers because they don't know how to shout at you, but Jeremy has said that if anyone is naughty then he is going to get them.

He already got Mario. All Mario did was laugh at the wrong time when Miss Crumble was reading a story.

He got Sam Lancer too. Sam was doing impressions of Miss Crumble, walking along behind her when she was going through the yard.

Jeremy said that Mario and Sam deserved a smack each. Then he gave them four smacks each, two on each ear.

When Miss Crumble asks questions, Jeremy puts his hand up and when she says, 'Yes, Jeremy?' he can hardly even answer. He says, 'Um' or something and just sits staring at her until she asks someone else.

Today he wore clean clothes to school and must have had his weekly wash three days early. Miss Crumble said to him, 'You're looking pretty cool today, Jeremy.' He gave her a bunch of flowers that he had hidden behind his back. He looked really silly.

'Oh, thank you Jeremy, they're lovely,' said Miss Crumble.

But they weren't lovely, they were only onion weed that he had picked in the vacant block next to his place. She put them in a vase and the room stank all day.

So we reckon that Jeremy is in love with her. But Jeremy says he's not and that he will get anyone who says he is.

We still reckon he is, but we're not going to say it. Not to him, anyway.

No one is in love with Mrs Smith because she is too old.

by Thadeus Antwerp

Yesterday, we had the grand opening of our new art room. Everybody assembled on the asphalt at one-fifteen. Seats had been arranged for parents, and there was an official table up the front for the invited guests to sit at. They were: our local Member of Parliament, Dr Thorndike, and his wife, as well as Mrs Chambers (Kathryn's mother) who is the president of the school council, and Mr Graves.

They all made speeches. Mr Graves went first and spoke for 10 minutes and 3.3 seconds. Then it was Mrs Chambers' turn. She had been going on for 14 minutes and 17.8 seconds when the whole line of grade-two boys fell over sideways and landed on each other's legs, making a lot of dust and noise. It took Miss Finly 5 minutes and 28.6 seconds to straighten them all up again and make them stop arguing about who pushed. Then it took Mr Monroe 3 minutes and 23.4 seconds to make the rest of the school keep quiet, even though he was using the loudspeaker.

Then Mrs Chambers took another 16 minutes and 0.3 of a second to finish her speech. After that it was Dr Thorndike's turn. He only took 2 minutes and 5.5 seconds, and everyone clapped for 9.4 seconds. Then he cut the ribbon across the door of the art room and Miss Martiner took them in for a guided tour.

While this was going on we had to sing the school song, then most of us had playtime early while the guests and teachers were served afternoon tea. Some of us, including Martin, David P and I, were required to act as waiters. I timed us all to see how fast we could serve a cup of tea and scones. Martin was fastest with 4.3 seconds. He also set the record for spilling the most, including some scones with jam and cream on Dr Thorndike's trousers.

I find my new quartz watch to be very useful. It has three alarms, a stop-watch function, the date, and the time in ten different zones. At the press of a button I can tell you what the time is in New York, London, Tokyo, Moscow and lots of other places. I think that's remarkable, don't you?

Boys' Germs

by Joan Smith

Today, grade six went to the high school for Orientation Day, so we went to grade six for the afternoon to meet next year's teacher. Guess who we're going to have. It's not hard because he's had grade six for the last five years, and he's been growing a beard all this year, and he wrote the school play. You're right, it's Mr Zeiner, and he made all the girls sit with boys and all the boys sit with girls.

I had to sit next to Mario Marati. He called me 'babe'. He said, 'How's it going, babe?' I wasn't going to answer him, so I just gave him a 'drop dead' look, and he clutched his throat and said, 'Aah, she's killing me.'

He is so childish.

Mr Z talked about what we'll be doing in grade six. It sounds a lot easier than grade five. We're going to do lots of writing, singing, and assignments about the environment. He didn't

even mention maths. My mother says that once you've learnt to read and write, then the only other useful subject is maths. She says that all other subjects are a waste of time. It looks like we're going to waste a lot of time next year.

Mr Z said that we're going to do drama, and he was pleased to see Mario acting already. He was making vomiting noises into his desk because I touched his arm, by mistake of course, and he said he had girls' germs on him. I'm going to disinfect myself as soon as I get home.

Mr Z said that when we come on the first day next year, we're to sit exactly where we sat today. There's no way that I'm ever going to sit beside Mario Marati again. I'm getting my mother to send me to a nice clean girls' school where everyone has to wear a uniform and teachers won't be allowed to have beards. Then I'll never get any boys' germs.

Kathryn said not to go within one metre of Mr Zeiner's beard, because things might be living in it and they can probably jump about ninety-five centimetres.

Carols by Candlelight

by Kathryn Chambers

Last night, we had our first ever Carols by Candlelight. It should have been really good, but some things went wrong.

Poor Miss Finly! She was standing next to Mr Zeiner when he set fire to his beard with a candle. Poor Mrs Smith! She was standing on the other side of him and had to put out the flames with her glass of raspberry cordial. They must have been so embarrassed.

Poor Mrs Graves! She had to pretend that she didn't know it was Mr Graves who was dressed up as Father Christmas. After Sylvia Karlos pulled his beard and the elastic broke then we all knew who it was.

It's lucky Mr Monroe doesn't have a wife, because if he did she would have been very embarrassed when he arrived dressed as a Blues Brother, and I don't think he should have brought his dogs, Rock and Roll, because Mrs Marso had already brought her poodle, Christmas Pudding. Rock and Roll are very bad mannered and my mother said they could do with a bucket of cold water thrown over them, and so could Mr Monroe.

It's no wonder that Mr Bollie isn't married, because he just doesn't know how to dress properly. He wore very short shorts and a T-shirt. That's not very religious, is it? My mother said that they just let anybody become a teacher these days.

Poor Mrs Flower (the RE teacher) tried to get everyone to sing Christmas carols but some people (boys mainly) kept singing the wrong words. It wasn't even funny.

If I were in charge, then I would have had the Police band instead of the Salvation Army band, because then they could have at least arrested people and caught Rock and Roll and put them in the pound.

by Martin Peters

We had Carols by Candlelight on the school oval last night. You should have been there. It was so funny. Mr Zeiner had been growing a beard all year, and he actually set it on fire with his own candle, right in the middle of Mr Graves' 'Challenge to the Future' speech.

Imagine this: Mr Graves is standing on the hill at the end of the oval, dressed as Father Christmas, talking about endangered possums, when Mr Zeiner's beard starts to smoulder. He didn't even notice, probably because he was asleep, until Mrs Smith threw her drink over him to put it out. That woke him up. Lots of people clapped and Mr Graves thought it was for his speech and said, 'Thank you, thank you,' and held his arms up as if he didn't deserve it, which he didn't. My dad asked if this was meant to be a comedy act and shouldn't they be on television.

After that, Mrs Flower tried to get us all to sing Christmas carols. She handed out word sheets, but we didn't need them because we made up our own words. We got them to rhyme and everything. We didn't sing too loudly though in case someone heard us. Kathryn Chambers and Joan Smith heard us and they really went off. They tried to kill us by yelling from their deck-chairs, but we're not scared of them.

Just when Kathryn's mother had started her 'Thanks to all the hardworking staff' speech, Mr Monroe's dogs, Rock and Roll, got away from the tree they were tied to, and tried to do it with Mrs Marso's poodle. That was much funnier than Mrs Chambers' speech. You should have seen Mrs Marso run.

After that, the grade sixers were supposed to sing the school song for the last time ever before going to high school. They have already sung it for the last time ever six times this week: once for their graduation dinner, once at the opening of the art room, and once every day for practice. This was the final last time but half the girls couldn't sing properly because they were crying.

Next year, we're going to be grade sixers. We'll be in charge of everything. No one will be able to tell us what to do. We'll be the biggest kids in the school. It'll be great.

KOALA HILLS PRIMARY SCHOOL

Newsletter no. 40   15th December

From Mr Graves, Principal

It was lovely to see so many parents, children and friends at the school for our inaugural Carols by Candlelight last night. We hope to make it an annual event, and in these times of uncertainty both at home and on the world stage, a little bit of community singing and prayer may in some way improve our situation.

Excellent, fete committee, excellent, excellent. I cannot over-emphasise what an excellent job you have done. Yes I know the fete was six weeks ago, and I have mentioned this in previous newsletters, but I must bring it up again because at last the new art room is finished, thanks to the money raised at the fete. What a wonderful day it was this week

Vice Principal Mrs Marso dishes out some delicious tropical punch for Dr. and Mrs Cyril Thorndike M.P.

when it was officially opened by our local MP, Dr Cyril Thorndike. What a superlative afternoon tea was put on by the Parents Club for our guests and how charming it was to see some senior students acting as waiters.

Martin, Thadeus and I did this . .

It is occasions like these that put our little school before the public, and I'd just like to say how proud I am of you all. Unfortunately the day was just a wee bit marred by a scuffle amongst the grade-two boys, however we expect that the nice long summer holiday will relieve their tensions before we have to face them in the new year.

I would just like to wish all the staff, children and parents a safe and happy Christmas, and I look forward to seeing you all fit and well in February.

WINNERS of the Parents Club Christmas raffle:

1st prize, the Christmas hamper worth $200, goes to lucky young Basil Antwerp. Don't eat it all at once, Bazza!

2nd prize, a piece of modern sculpture called *Desperation* made by local artist, Mr John Pierce, valued at $150, goes to our school librarian, Mr Bob Jergens, who is fully recovered and will be back with us next year.

3rd prize, a video of the school production, 'Princess Confetti and the Space-Ace', filmed by Mr John Smith of 10 Pleasant Crescent was won by Mr John Smith. Copies are available from Mr Smith for a small fee. 731 66702

Thadeus has bought three copies because he wants to look at Princess Confetti over and over again. He thought if he only had one copy it might wear out.

HELP WANTED

The school council wants help with watering the gardens and oval over the Christmas break. Please contact Mrs Lawson, to volunteer. 732 89105

ADVERTISEMENTS

For Sale: *Recession Recipes*, a cookbook produced by the Parents Club with contributions by members of the school community. Was $5, now only $3.50.

Martin is going to give one to Mrs Smith. I don't think she'll like it.

For Sale: Baby lizards. They make great Christmas presents. 95 cents each. Contact Martin Peters, or his brother.

I gave one to Mary (my girlfriend). She'll like it. I only had to pay 50 cents because Martin is my friend.

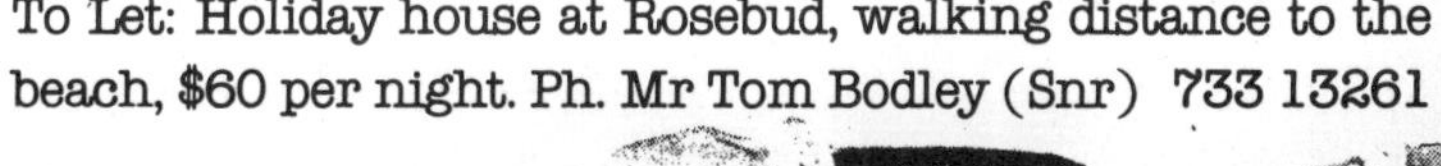

To Let: Holiday house at Rosebud, walking distance to the beach, $60 per night. Ph. Mr Tom Bodley (Snr) 733 13261

Do you suffer from headaches, tension, muscular aches and pains? Contact Mrs Dean for a massage. Prompt and personal attention guaranteed. 756 90324

Have you been recessed by the recession, depressed by the depression? Has the bank confiscated your card? Contact Mr P Antwerp for full financial advice. 732 68127

From the Author

'I live in Melbourne with my husband and two children. I have been a primary teacher since 1974, and have worked in many schools as an emergency teacher since 1981.

'Teachers and children say and do lots of funny things which I have used for the stories in *It's Not Fair!*. I hope they didn't notice me noticing them. Maybe you are in this book.'

From the Illustrator

'I live in Adelaide with Lisa and our two children, Hannah and Huw. I have been doing drawings for children's books for some years now and it remains, I believe, the best fun you can have with a pen, paint and paper.

'I've loved the opportunity to return to Koala Hills, taking my pen and pencil set, and meeting up with the kids there again.'

THERE'S NUFFIN' LIKE A PUFFIN!

☆☆

I Hate Fridays Rachel Flynn/Illustrated by Craig Smith

A collection of stories about characters in the classroom, about all the funny, sad and traumatic things that can happen. Hilariously illustrated by the very popular Craig Smith.

A Children's Book Council of Australia Notable Book, 1991.

I Can't Wait! Rachel Flynn/Illustrated by Craig Smith

It's the last year of primary school for the characters from Koala Hills. Following the huge success of *I Hate Fridays* and *It's Not Fair!*, here are your favourite characters back again.

Worried Sick Rachel Flynn/Illustrated by Craig Smith

The characters from Koala Hills have now entered the minefield of secondary school in this, the fourth book in the hugely successful I Hate Fridays series.

The Lenski Kids and Dracula Libby Hathorn/Illustrated by Peter Viska

The Lenski kids are the wildest, naughtiest kids in the neighbourhood – until Kim Kip arrives next door. She goes to acting school and is saving for a Harley Davidson motor bike, and is keen to do some babysitting . . .

THERE'S NUFFIN' LIKE A PUFFIN!

☆☆

So Who Needs Lotto? Libby Hathorn/Illustrated by Simon Kneebone

When Denise Albermarle arrives at Mimosa Primary School, she is such a show-off and a bully that everyone hates her. So when she begins to strike up a friendship with shy Cosmo Ravezzi, no one is more surprised than he is . . .

A Children's Book Council of Australia Notable Book, 1991.

Britt the Boss Margaret Clark/
Illustrated by Bettina Guthridge

You might know some bossy people, but no one compares to Bossy Boots Britt at Mango Street Primary! Here's another hilarious story about everyone's favourite group of kids.

Wally the Whiz Kid Margaret Clark/
Illustrated by Bettina Guthridge

There's this kid in the class who's a real brain. Wally is super-intelligent, but he manages to get into some pretty complicated situations in this very funny Mango Street Story.

Butterfingers Margaret Clark/Illustrated by Bettina Guthridge

It isn't much fun being the clumsiest kid at Mango Street Primary School. Stacey 'Butterfingers' Martin sure has a problem, and it's a real hassle for everyone, especially Mandy. But after they go to the fun park for Mandy's birthday, something *very* weird happens.

THERE'S NUFFIN' LIKE A PUFFIN!

☆☆

The Twenty-Seventh Annual African Hippopotamus Race
Morris Lurie/Illustrated by Elizabeth Honey

Eight-year-old Edward trains very hard for this greatest of swimming marathons with no idea of the cunning and jealousy he'll meet from the other competitors. This best-selling story takes you behind the scenes and shows you just what it takes to become a champion.

Winner of the Young Australians' Best Book Award (YABBA) 1986.

Invasion of the Monsters Paul J. Shaw

What do you do when monsters become real? When vampires advertise coffins on TV? Well, Ant and Cleo decide to call in Basil Kufflock, a retired monster-hunter. And what a wild, weird, wacky adventure that turns out to be!

Sit Down, Mum, There's Something I've Got To Tell You Moya Simons

A funny, fast-moving story about Hatty, a teenage girl who thinks her mum needs a love-life after her divorce. Hatty decides to arrange one, with hilarious results!

Turn Right For Zyrgon Robin Klein

The funny and totally unexpected antics of that weird family from Zyrgon continue. This time, they return to their home planet and find that things aren't quite the same any more.